COMPELLING URGES

Compelling Urges

ARIELLA TALIX

Ringmaster Publishing

Cover design by: CIF
Photos by Valua Vitaly and Konrad Bak
ISBN: 979-8-9856766-4-8

Library of Congress Control Number: TXu 2-268-192

"The feeling of facing the unknown and trying something for the first time can give you a thrilling adrenaline kick, and for some people, arousal is connected to that feeling of adrenaline."

- Cassandra Corrado, Sex Educator

Chapter One

Cooper Houston glared at the piece of paper he'd found propped up next to the cold, empty coffeemaker. He grabbed it and wadded it up in his hand angrily. It was a letter from Bodhi, his roommate and best friend in the world—or at least he *had* been Cooper's best friend.

The wad had been a good-bye message to him and to Ivy, who still lay asleep in Bodhi's bed, blissfully unaware that the floor had just dropped out from under them.

Cooper thought better of his actions and smoothed out the letter. It was, after all, addressed to both of them, and he had no right to deprive Ivy the dubious pleasure of reading it. He placed it on the counter again.

"What a miserable jerk," he muttered as he stomped down the hall. Cooper had been out all night enjoying the company of a lovely lady. *Mindy? Mandy?* He wasn't sure, but it didn't matter anyway. He came home hoping for a cup of coffee and a quick chat with Bodhi before heading to his office. As usual, Ivy was sleeping in. She didn't work on Mondays and often went back to her apartment after Bodhi left for work.

Cooper had a bad habit of seeking the company of anonymous women. They provided him with a temporary distraction from his true desire, which was so impossible and shocking that he could barely admit it to himself.

When Ivy had first appeared on Bodhi's arm and began keeping company with him, Cooper burned with jealousy. Ivy seemed so perfect in every way, and he wondered routinely if Bodhi appreciated her...

But the jealousy ran deeper than that. It wasn't just that he wanted Ivy for himself. He wanted Bodhi, too. It confused him no end, so he trolled for women and sought relief in meaning-less hook-ups. The relief was only fleeting.

After showering and changing into fresh clothes, Cooper realized the house was still quiet; Ivy wasn't up yet. Figuring she may need some moral support for what she was about to discover, he steeled himself and knocked lightly on Bodhi's bedroom door. No answer. He tried again and waited. Still nothing. So, he opened the door and discovered Ivy spread out in Bodhi's bed on her stomach, sound asleep. Her black cascade of hair covered most of her bare back, but the sheet was pulled down enough to reveal the cute dimples just above her round bottom. *My god, she's exquisite*, he thought to himself for the umpteenth time. How could Bodhi up and leave some-one so fine and so sweet? He also couldn't stomach that Bodhi had left *him,* and the pain was like a knife to the gut.

"Ivy?" he asked softly. Still no response. He could hear her light snores as she slept on. Cooper sat down on the edge of the bed and gently lay his hand in the middle of her golden, tanned back. She felt like warm silk. "Ivy? Wake up. I need to talk to you."

Blinking, Ivy dragged herself up slowly. Cooper got an eyeful of her bodacious tatas before she realized who was there and just how naked she was. With an embarrassed gasp, she snatched up the sheet to cover herself. "What's going on, Cooper? Why are you in here? What time is it? Why aren't you dressed for work?"

Cooper's brows knit and his jaw flexed before he blurted, "Bodhi's gone. He left us."

"What? What do you mean he left us?" Ivy's dark brown eyes went huge.

"Maybe you should put on some clothes for this. I'll be in the kitchen. He left us a note." Cooper strode from the room thinking that his office was the last place he wanted to be this morning, but home wasn't a lot better.

* * *

Ivy kept a few things at Bodhi's place. When she opened the closet to grab something, she found that Cooper was right: Bodhi's clothes were all gone. Every last piece.

A throbbing pain in her head reminded Ivy how much she and Bodhi had drunk the night before. Or anyway, she had assumed he was as drunk as she was... now, thinking more carefully, she remembered Bodhi filling her glass over and over with tequila, and she remembered him telling her to take a shot for this reason, then take a shot for that reason, but she didn't remember him actually drinking much at all. *The rat!* She also had a hazy recollection of doing a silly striptease for Bodhi... and that was it. Did he get her drunk so he could secretly pack and sneak away? Apparently so. Seething with anger, she jerked on her clothes.

She grabbed some aspirin and went in search of Cooper, who she found making coffee and telling someone on his phone, "I just wanted to let you know that my schedule isn't too bad today so I won't be in. I need to take a personal day. Yeah. No, I don't need help, but thanks for offering."

Cooper was an attorney in a small private office with his father and older sister. He took his responsibilities seriously. Ivy couldn't remember him ever calling out for a personal day before. He must be just as shaken by Bodhi's disappearance as she was. As Cooper finished his call, Ivy reached for the wrinkled piece of paper on the counter.

Dear Ivy and Cooper,

Guess what? I've been offered the job of my dreams, and I am leaving today for London, England. Isn't that great?

They asked me to head up the London branch of the finance firm, and it's an offer I can't refuse. This will make my career. I don't expect I'll be back.

Sorry I didn't tell you both sooner, but I didn't have much time to think about it. They gave me the offer and said it was immediate.

Ivy, I know we haven't known each other that long, but you are very special to me, and I'll never forget you. I know, however, that your gallery is important to you, and I wouldn't have felt right asking you to leave it. I'm sure you'll find a new boyfriend soon. I wish you success in everything.

Cooper, you're the best. When I met you during grad school, and we hit it off the way we did, I knew you were destined to be my friend for life. I'll miss you. You can always come and visit if your busy schedule ever lets up and you have a break. I'll send an address when I'm settled.

Please stay in the house, Cooper. I paid cash, as you know, so there isn't any mortgage. If you keep paying the taxes and maintain the property, there is no reason to pay me rent. The house is a great investment, and I don't have plans to sell it.

Let me know how things are going from
time to time. I had to leave my boards. Man,
I'll miss surfing with you. But... duty calls!

Best of luck to both of you.
Cheerio! (Do they really say that?)
Bodhi Monaghan

"Do you think he used his full name because he thought we forgot it already?" Ivy asked. She was trying to be funny, but her voice cracked as she said it. "What a raging asshole! I told him I loved him, and this is how he treats me? And what's this business about not knowing each other for very long? I can't believe this; we've been dating for months!" Tears streamed down her face as she stared down at the note.

Cooper wrapped his strong arms around her. Ivy leaned into him and sobbed into his chest. For a moment, Cooper considered that his clean shirt would likely be covered in tears and snot when she was done, but he dismissed the concern almost as fast as he thought of it. *What the hell,* he thought. *I'll just change again. And honestly... she feels damn good in my arms.*

"Let's go sit down on the couch, Ivy. Here, let me grab you a cup of coffee."

"I loved him," she wept into his chest.

"Did he ever say it back to you?" Cooper asked thoughtlessly.

After a long sniffle, she answered hoarsely, "He usually changed the subject or said something funny to deflect."

"Sounds like Bodhi. But up until he pulled this bullshit stunt today, I'd have bet my life on it that he loved you. He was always talking about you when you weren't around."

This brought on a new wave of sobs.

Cooper felt like crying, too, but kept his man card intact by being the comforter rather than the comforted. *How could Bodhi do this?* he wondered over and over. The idea of Bodhi being gone for good gutted him. The fact that he'd been secretive about it felt like pouring acid into the open wound. And that note... it was so casual. No remorse or concern. As if they hadn't mattered to him at all.

Throughout the day, he and Ivy trashed the memory of her lover and his best buddy over and over in more and more creative ways. They ended up starving by the afternoon and headed out for a giant Mexican meal in the barrio. It was the best comfort food in the world. Cooper offered to get them margaritas.

"Oh, ugh. No thanks," Ivy answered with a shudder. "I may never drink tequila again."

* * *

Cooper was exhausted both mentally and physically after the night of frivolity with Mindy/Mandy and the subsequent day of drama he'd had with Ivy, so they made it back to the house fairly early. Ivy had planned to drive her car home from there, but it turned out she didn't feel much like being alone. Cooper immediately picked up on her reluctance to leave and offered to let her stay the night. She agreed without hesitation.

She was used to sleeping in Bodhi's magnificent bed, but it felt huge, cold, and lonely now. After tossing and turning for a while, she wandered down the hall to Cooper's room. She was tired of crying; she needed a diversion or some more of his company—something to occupy her thoughts. His door was ajar, so she stepped inside, but once through the threshold, Ivy found herself hesitating. She wasn't quite sure what she wanted from Cooper.

Cooper and Bodhi were both athletic. They'd met each other when they joined a beach volleyball team during Cooper's second year of law school and Bodhi's last year of grad school. They soon discovered that they were both avid surfers, and they began to spend more and more time together. Eventually, they became roommates, renting an apartment together until Bodhi made enough money to buy the Del Mar house where they now lived—a three-bedroom house on a hillside above the water with a fantastic view of the ocean. It was convenient to both of their offices, and they were delighted with it. They each took a bedroom and turned the third into a home gym where they worked out when the surf was lousy.

Standing in the doorway, Ivy admired Cooper's bare chest and his thick biceps—a beautifully toned surfer's body. His hair gleamed with a hundred shades of red and brown when the sun hit it, but in the moonlight, it just looked soft and inviting. She'd always harbored a secret crush on Bodhi's best friend, but of course, she knew enough to keep that to herself.

Creeping into the room, her toe knocked into one of the shoes Cooper had carelessly left in the middle of the floor. "Ow!" she exclaimed far more loudly than she intended. Cooper jolted upright with a startled look on his face. "I'm so sorry, Cooper," Ivy said in an unnecessary whisper. She turned to leave and tripped over his other shoe. "Ow, oh crud." She started to sniffle again. It was so typical of Cooper to leave his stuff laying around; she should have been more careful.

Seeing her retreating form, Cooper called out, "Ivy, come back. What's wrong? Are you okay?" She turned to look at him, and he could see telltale streaks of tears on her cheeks glistening in the moonlight. She looked like an angel in her diaphanous nightgown. "Do you need some company tonight?" He held out a large hand toward her as if to draw her back to him.

It didn't take any more encouragement than that. She sprinted to the bed, carefully hopping over the wayward shoes and pounced onto the bed just as Cooper drew down the covers for her to slide in. It felt perfect to snuggle into Cooper's broad chest and feel his warm embrace anchoring her to him.

"I feel like I'll shatter into a million pieces if you don't hold me together right now," she whispered. "Thank you."

Cooper chuckled. "Holding you is no hardship, believe me." In fact, he thought, holding Ivy did a lot to make him feel like his world was improving. He chanced a few kisses on the top of her head as she nestled into his bare chest.

And thus, it began. They spent more and more time together over the next days, weeks, and months, and they went from friends to lovers as naturally as breathing. Hugging and kisses on the cheek evolved into more and more passionate embraces, and when they finally had sex the first time, it was as comfortable as it was thrilling. They found in each other a hunger for going beyond the normal vanilla, and they soon incorporated toys and games. Sex was never routine for Cooper and Ivy.

They eventually professed their love to one another, and their affection was true and deep. However, neither admitted that Bodhi's exit from their lives still left a gaping wound. They acted as if they were over it, but in truth, it still chafed and burned. Ivy rarely spoke of him, and Cooper only mentioned him now and then when he got a quick text from Bodhi. They did invoke his name, however, in a little game they played. It was meant as an insult... possibly.

Cooper secretly worried that *he* was the real reason Bodhi left. Had Bodhi gotten sick of his moony-eyed glances? Did he want to get away from Cooper's weird fixation on him? Did he catch sight of his ill-timed boners now and then? Cooper had tried to hide them, and one time when it was painfully obvious, he'd laughed it off by explaining he'd been thinking about his last date. Lies. All lies. But the attraction never made any sense to Cooper; he'd been one hundred percent heterosexual until Bodhi came into his life. Now...? The confusion was compounded by Bodhi's abandonment. Cooper's solution was to bury his need and throw himself completely into making Ivy feel cherished.

Bodhi was gone. Ivy was here. Cooper needed to feel complete with that knowledge, so that's what he told himself to do.

Chapter Two

A Year Later

Cooper held up a sparkling ring as he knelt in the sand. Around them, the sky was streaked with hues of pink, purple, and orange in the glorious sunset. It was the perfect setting for his proposal.

But before Cooper could pop the question, a large wave crashed over them. The heirloom ring was swept from his hand by the frigid Pacific Ocean.

"It's gone! Help me find it, Ivy! My grandmother's ring!" Cooper scrambled around scooping futilely at the churning water as it receded. "Help me!" Then to his added horror, he saw that the wave had also swept Ivy away, and she was being dragged out to sea. Away from him.

* * *

Groggily, Ivy sat up in bed wondering what had woken her. She looked at Cooper as he thrashed around in his sleep. He seemed to be trying to say something, but whatever it was, it was garbled. It sounded like, "Hep." His hands were twitching, and he seemed to be in distress, so she gently lay her hand on his arm and stroked his bicep.

Ivy bit her lip with worry. Cooper had clearly been on edge about something all night before they went to bed, so she wasn't too surprised at his restless sleep. "Wake up, Cooper. You're dreaming," she said softly. When nothing happened except for more "hep" noises, she shook him a little and leaned over to speak right into his ear. "It's okay, honey. You're dreaming. Wake up."

With a desperate gasp, Cooper bolted up and stared wildly around the room for a couple of seconds. Completely discombobulated, he finally focused his eyes on Ivy and then grabbed for her left hand. When he saw the diamond shining in the dim light of pre-dawn, he let out a gigantic sigh of relief. "Ohmygod, I was so scared, Ivy." He wrapped his arms around her and dragged her to his chest. The solid warmth of her body against his comforted him.

Ivy let him relax for a moment before she asked, "Do you mind if I close the window? It's suddenly gotten colder than normal in here." When he loosened his grip on her, she slipped off the bed and cranked the pane shut. "Phew, that's better. The June gloom is kind of chilly tonight." She slid back in next to Cooper, who had an odd look on his face. "What's wrong?" she asked.

Cooper choked out, "I thought I'd lost you."

"Oh, that must have felt terrible, but I'm right here. Everything's fine. It was just a bad dream. Maybe your stomach was upset by the spicy food we had for dinner." She kissed his cheek and rubbed his arm. He was shivering slightly and covered with goose bumps.

Letting out a colossal sigh, Cooper responded, "I need to tell you something."

Narrowing her eyes at him, she asked, "What? I have the feeling I might not like this."

Cooper huffed and mumbled, "We'll see." He drew her to his chest where he could feel her but didn't have to look into her eyes. "I... ah... got a text."

"Yeah? And?"

"It was from Bodhi."

"Well, that's not too scary. He sends you messages now and then, doesn't he?"

Cooper rubbed his chin and pulled on his ear before continuing. Clearly, this was hard for him for some reason she couldn't fathom. Finally, he said quietly, "He's coming back."

"Um, okay. For a visit?" Ivy's voice was a bit unsteady.

"No. He's moving home." The rest of Cooper's words tumbled out finally, "He'll be here in a few hours."

Ivy lurched back and asked, "What? Why didn't you tell me? This could get to be awfully uncomfortable. I'm going to have to find another place to live right away."

"Maybe not. Maybe we can all get along."

Ivy snorted. "Yeah, right. How would you like to live in the same house as your ex? He's obviously going to move back in since the house belongs to him. I thought he said he was leaving permanently. What happened?"

"Sorry, I have absolutely no idea. His text just said that he'd be here around noon and he's back for good. I texted him back for more information, and all he said was, 'Lots to talk about when I see you.'"

"I don't understand why you didn't tell me as soon as you got his text. How long have you known about this?"

Cooper hung his head for a moment and then looked imploringly into Ivy's eyes. "He texted me from the London airport— probably because it was too late for me to try to convince him not to come. It's been several hours now, so he's probably already in the air. I know I should have told you, but I was so afraid of losing you to him when he gets back, I couldn't deal with it. I pushed it to the back of my mind and hoped it would just stay there. I love you so much, Ivy. And Bodhi is so charismatic. I just... panicked and clammed up. Not one of my better moves. I'm sorry. Please don't be angry with me."

"You're right about it not being one of your better moves, but I guess I can understand your panic." She sighed and shook her head. "I'm not going to stop loving you because Bodhi is around. That's kind of silly. He deserted me, and I'm still furious with him about that."

"Well, there's something about Bodhi that you like, or we wouldn't have invoked his name in bed so often. I know it was a joke, but still..."

Ivy covered her face with her hands and moaned. "I knew it was a bad idea to pretend he was part of our little game. I won't be able to look the man in the face. And you have to promise me faithfully, Cooper, that you'll never tell him."

"I wouldn't dream of it. How do you think he'd feel if I told him that he was a fantasy member of our threesome, and we have a weird-looking dildo we call Bodhi?" He shook his head. "I'd laugh if it weren't so strange."

Ivy laughed and snuggled closer to Cooper. He was relieved that she had forgiven him for keeping Bodhi's return to himself, but his worries were far from over. It gnawed on him that Ivy and Bodhi had unresolved feelings for each other, and despite her assurances, he feared that he stood a good chance of losing her. The thought made him miserable. He knew she'd been deeply in love with Bodhi, but he was afraid to delve too deeply into how she felt about the man now. Being furious with someone usually meant they still meant something to you, didn't it? It was possible she still loved him. Plus, there were also *his* unresolved feelings for Bodhi. Life was going to become terribly complicated—and soon.

Chapter Three

Ivy Chambers had grown up in the Chicago area and always hated the dreary, cold winters. When she was old enough to leave for college, she chose UCSD in La Jolla, not only because it was a great university, but also for its climate and proximity to the ocean. It was the perfect choice for her. She felt herself come alive in the year-round sunny climate and adored everything about the area. She never considered leaving after graduation, so when an opportunity arose to go to work in an upscale art gallery in Del Mar, she jumped at the chance. The gazillionaire owner became so fond of Ivy that when he wanted to retire after working with her for five years, he transferred the ownership of the gallery to her for a nominal buyout. Ivy's extensive knowledge of the art world, as well as her business acumen, helped her continue the business profitably even while art sales were soft elsewhere.

One of the most enjoyable duties she performed as the business owner was searching for new artists whom she felt needed a gallery presence. Unlike the previous owner who'd stuck to the tried-and-true, she had feelers out to all the major art schools in the country, and she often took a chance on new artists. Not all of her exhibits were total successes, but she had an impressive track record. She also routinely heard from agents who wanted to showcase their clients' work. Del Mar was an upscale town, so buyers were plentiful, and the gallery's reputation spread all over Southern California.

Ivy's personal taste in art was eclectic, but when she discovered a young man from Redondo Beach who specialized in surfing art, she thought she'd struck gold. The guy was a genius with a paintbrush, and she couldn't wait to make a killing with his gorgeous work. There were many professionals in San Diego County who loved to surf. With that in mind, she organized a show for him as quickly as possible and promoted it heavily throughout the area.

Normally, her buyers were older, well-heeled couples, but this time the art opening attracted a younger crowd. The paintings were relatively reasonable in price due to the artist's lack of reputation, so sales that night were brisk. She knew it was just a matter of time before the value of his work skyrocketed, and she was ready to plan the next exhibit for him then.

Ivy and her assistant kept busy throughout the opening party with sale after sale, but one buyer made her stop and stare for longer than was polite. A tall, beautifully built young man about her age stood grinning at her as he produced his credit card to buy the largest, most expensive painting in the show. He had a shock of thick, sun-streaked golden hair, a naughty smile, and sparkling hazel eyes. The cleft in his chin made her want to nibble his face, and that thought made her blush to the roots of her ebony hair. The name on the card he produced was Bodhi Monaghan.

Noticing the blush as well as her incredible beauty, Bodhi asked her, "Where have you been all my life? Please make me a happy man and let me take you out for a late dinner when you're done here." His voice was deep and felt like a caress to her ears.

Stammering, Ivy answered, "Uh...absolutely." She shocked herself with her quick reply, but this guy was definitely something special. She couldn't remember ever being so attracted to anyone... ever.

Ivy tried to play it cool over the next few weeks with Bodhi, but their physical need for each other was off the charts. She began spending more and more nights at his place rather than at her little apartment in nearby Solana Beach, and she knew after a few short months that she was deeply in love with him. He was smart, generous, funny, and as sexy a man as she'd ever encountered.

There were only two things that kept life with Bodhi from being perfect. The first was his housemate Cooper. The first time Ivy met him, the same visceral feeling of attraction barreled through her that she'd felt for Bodhi. It worried her. *How can I be so attracted to two men at the same time? Am I kidding myself about my feelings for Bodhi?* she wondered, but then she tried to boot the attraction out of her mind. The second hitch in her happiness came from Bodhi himself. Ivy had strong feelings for him—feelings that she was ready to express. One night, after he'd been exceptionally attentive and careful with their lovemaking, Ivy decided it was time. He'd blown her mind and her heart simultaneously, and she had every reason to think he felt the same way about her.

"Bodhi?" she asked softly.

"Hmm?" he purred into her neck as he caressed her bottom.

"I love you."

No sooner were the words out of her mouth than she wanted to haul them back in with heavy-loading equipment and a giant memory-erasing spell. She felt his body stiffen and he cleared his throat.

Nothing came out of Bodhi's mouth for a while. Long enough, in fact, that she tried to convince herself he hadn't heard her. Then he asked, "Want something to drink? I'm thirsty." When she shook her head, he leapt up and sprinted to the kitchen. He apparently needed fresh-squeezed orange juice or something equally labor-intensive because he didn't come back for a solid fifteen minutes. When he did, he asked her, "Want to watch a movie?" Apparently, that was the end of the "feelings" discussion.

And then a few months after that, Bodhi disappeared from her life as though she'd meant nothing. The pain devastated her.

* * *

Now a year later, Ivy definitely loved Cooper, but she also couldn't deny some leftover feelings toward Bodhi. Marrying Cooper and establishing a happy life with him seemed the best course of action—one that would erase those lingering cravings for a man who'd forsaken her. When Cooper proposed, Ivy took her feelings for Bodhi and locked them securely away in a vault somewhere in the back of her brain. She wanted to move forward with her life rather than wallow in what might have been. Bodhi had hurt her, and there was no turning back.

Chapter Four

Bodhi Monaghan was a brilliant financier, especially for a young man of only twenty-nine. He'd gone to work for a boutique investment company that acknowledged his incredible talents within a couple of years and offered him the chance to go to London where he could head up their office there. Their offer felt more like an order, but he decided it was an amazing opportunity for him, and he was flattered by the idea of the increased responsibility. He convinced himself that his career advancement ought to be the most important thing in his life.

Unfortunately, he should have given more consideration to his relationship with Ivy Chambers—the woman he'd met in an art gallery she owned in Del Mar. Her shapely little body made his blood boil. He loved to wrap her magnificent black waves around his fist as he made insatiable love to her. Her enormous brown eyes, so dark they appeared almost black, seemed to see into his very soul, and he often found himself lost in them. Ivy's fiery spirit attracted him to her like no woman ever had, and the feelings he had for her shook him to the core. Beyond the immense physical attraction he felt, he also recognized that she was a shrewd businesswoman with a quick mind that he respected tremendously.

He just wasn't ready for a serious relationship, no matter how hard he'd fallen for her.

The prospect of moving to London didn't leave him with too many doubts—at least at first. He reasoned to himself that Ivy would get over him in time. He had to kid himself about his feelings for her so that he could make a clean break. The pain of leaving her cut him like a knife, but he tried to convince himself he was doing them both a favor. He knew it was a dick move to leave without saying a proper goodbye. But London was happening either way. The breakup was happening either way. He might as well not add pain to the process too. He thought that if he told himself over and over that he'd done the right thing, it would become the truth.

Bodhi also felt terrible about leaving Cooper behind. He had always enjoyed the heck out of Cooper's company, but once they were both living in the ocean view house, their friendship grew even stronger.

Over time, however, Bodhi realized he was feeling things for Cooper that were unfamiliar. Even though it did nothing to diminish his attraction to Ivy, Bodhi was aware he felt a longing he'd never felt before. It freaked him the fuck out. It was just one more good reason to skedaddle off to England as far as he was concerned.

Bodhi may have been brilliant when it came to business, but when it came to his personal matters, he was starting to realize that he was still immature and confused. His actions had hurt two people he cared about deeply. Even all the way in London, he couldn't seem to escape the guilt.

* * *

Bodhi's plane to Los Angeles got in early. He was jetlagged and exhausted by the time he finally landed, but going through customs went faster than usual, so he was able to jump on an earlier connection to San Diego and not wait around the LA airport for hours. Grabbing an Uber, he headed north, barely able to keep his eyes open. He imagined the feel of the smooth sheets in his old bed. *I'm so glad to be back*, he thought to himself as he drew in deep gulps of ocean air. It smelled like home.

The traffic wasn't too crazy since it was Sunday morning, so they made good time as they headed north to the seaside town of Del Mar.

"Are you a race fan?" asked the driver.

"Huh?" Bodhi didn't feel like talking, and his head had begun to throb.

"The Del Mar race track. I thought maybe since you live there, you like to play the ponies."

"Oh... no, not particularly." Bodhi closed his eyes. "If you don't mind, I'm going to take a nap." Bodhi adored going to the track during race season, but he absolutely didn't want to get into a conversation about it with this guy. He'd even toyed with the idea of buying some racehorses someday, although he knew he needed to do a lot of research before taking on that venture.

Bodhi had done some tremendously successful investing for his clients, and in turn his own financial status was solid—especially for his age. His own altruistic goals rested more in making his clients wealthy by his efforts than in making a ton of money for himself. His need to succeed for others seemed to be his own measure of success. However, his increasing income offered welcome benefits.

When they pulled up to his house, Bodhi shuffled through the gate to the front door, dragging his luggage behind him. He'd actually left a lot at his flat in London, and eventually he'd need to sort things out with that lease and get more of his possessions, but for now, he was happy to be back in sunny California and away from his troubles.

Looking around, he realized the yard had some great new landscaping and the house was freshly painted. It looked fantastic.

He used his key and dumped his stuff just inside the front door, shuffling his way down the hall to his bedroom. The closer he got, the more he imagined lying down in that wonderful bed and sleeping for about twelve straight hours. Entering his room, however, he came face-to-face with a sight he never expected. Cooper lay in the middle of his rumpled bed, crooning happily to a woman who was bent over his dick and giving Cooper one helluva blowjob. Her dark cascade of waves obstructed Bodhi's view of her face, but her luscious body was on full naked display, and despite his astonishment, Bodhi went titanium-hard immediately.

"What the fuck, Cooper?" he shouted. "Why are you in *my bed* with... shit!" The woman sat up and revealed herself with a look of shock. "Ivy?" Bodhi gaped at them and spluttered, "And why are you with *my girlfriend*?"

"Oh no you don't, Bodhi, you... snake!'" she hissed at him. "You dumped me a year ago and never sent so much as a birthday card or a lousy text message. I am not *your* anything! How dare you?"

"Well, this is my house and you're in my bed!"

"Wrong again, asshole. You left the house in my care, and you never said I couldn't use the largest room with the best view. Of course, I moved in here. You said you weren't coming back!" Cooper glared at his friend. His pale blue eyes bore into Bodhi's hazel ones with unchecked emotion. "How do you think we felt when you abandoned us? Did you ever think of anyone but yourself? At least using the master bedroom was some consolation. And why are you back so early?"

* * *

Throughout this entire exchange, for some reason, Ivy kept her fist wrapped tightly around Cooper's erection, and he stayed hard. Most men would have gone limp when being confronted this way, but Cooper seemed to... like it? Ivy glanced down and could see that not only was Cooper still hard, but he was also squeezing his ass and pumping his hips rhythmically into her fist. The movement was subtle, but it was there.

The other odd thing she noticed was that Bodhi may have sounded put out and angry, but the bulge in his pants told another story. She knew she ought to cover herself, but Bodhi had seen every inch of her already, so false modesty seemed childish to her. She had half a mind to continue Cooper's BJ so Bodhi could see what he missed out on.

Then she decided, *What the hell?* And she went for it. Keeping her eyes locked on Bodhi's, she leaned back down and engulfed Cooper with her mouth. Her eyes spoke volumes of "take that, asshole" vibes as she moaned happily over Cooper and resumed her energetic sucking and pumping.

Bodhi stood slack-jawed in the doorway as though rooted to the spot.

Soon Cooper cried out, "I'm gonna come!"

Ivy raised up and sat back.

Cooper let out a war cry as ropes of cum shot straight up, splashing on Ivy's chest and his belly. Creamy liquid dripped all over her hand while she continued to jack him off.

Bodhi's face went beet red. Then he spun on his heels and headed back down the hall. Within seconds, they heard a string of muttered curses and then a bedroom door slammed.

Chapter Five

"Well, that was awkward," Cooper laughed as he cleaned up with a handful of tissues. "Thanks for not leaving me with blue balls, though."

"You liked that a lot, didn't you?" She eyed Cooper's face for any signs he'd try to deny his excitement. Much to her surprise, it had turned her on immensely to have Bodhi watch them. "I don't think you felt awkward at all. 'Fess up. It got you off, didn't it?"

Shrugging, Cooper admitted, "Yeah, I'm not really sure why, but it kinda did. I don't know what his problem is and why he suddenly thinks everything is his, including you, but I have to admit, I loved having him watch you do that to me. I haven't come that hard in... well... ever."

"Do you think he'll want to kick us out now? We should probably think about getting our own place if he wants this house to himself again," Ivy mused.

"Let's not worry about that right now," Cooper chuckled. "Lie back and let me have a taste. We can pretend he's still watching while I eat you out. And if you want, we can use the Bodhi dildo too. It'll be even more fun now."

"You're so bad," she laughed, but instead of disagreeing, she reached into the bedside drawer and pulled out their favorite toy they'd irreverently named "Little Bodhi." It was a strangely beautiful glass anal dildo with a phallus on one end and a butt plug on the other. Then she grabbed some lube and handed them both to Cooper. "Do your best," she said with a wink. She was practically vibrating with eagerness for what she knew Cooper could do with his mouth, fingers, and a toy.

Cooper didn't disappoint her in the least. After kissing her body from top to bottom, he settled his mouth onto her clit. He licked and sucked her into a writhing mess before sitting back. Ivy gave a disappointed moan when he stopped his ministrations, but her eyes darkened with desire as she watched him quickly lube up the dildo.

"Spread your legs and raise up your hips for me," he crooned. Slowly and deliberately, he pressed the dildo onto her rosebud. He swiveled it around gently and then pushed it into her.

Ivy cried out, "Bodhi!" and then she got the giggles.

"Shh! Don't be so naughty! Do you want him to hear you?" Cooper laughed with a sly look.

"Maybe," she replied. "Ohh, don't stop, Cooper. That feels *so good.*"

Cooper leaned back down and sucked her clit back into his mouth with a chuckle, then he slipped two fingers inside of her as he continued to probe her bottom with the dildo.

"God, you're good at that," she groaned. She couldn't keep still as the feeling of her impending orgasm grew and grew. Her hips thrashed and her legs stiffened, and finally, the dam broke. All of the most wonderful sensations a body can feel swept through her like a tsunami. Wave after wave of profound pleasure took over as she bucked and spasmed. It was glorious.

"You're so beautiful when you come like that, Ivy. I love you so much." Cooper slowly extracted the dildo and wrapped it in a tissue from the bedside table where he set it down, then he slid up, covered them with the sheet and blanket and engulfed her in a full-body embrace. Within moments they were fast asleep again. It had been a long week and an emotional early morning. Dealing with Bodhi—and Little Bodhi—could wait.

Chapter Six

Down the hall from them, Bodhi stripped to his boxers and flung himself onto the bed he thought of as Cooper's. Then he remembered his suitcase, so he got up and wandered toward the foyer to grab it, figuring his lack of dress didn't matter much. Before he could make it back into the bedroom, he heard Ivy's voice cry out his name. He'd have gone to investigate, but it was followed up with laughter. His insides burned with shame and confusion as he flopped onto the bed for a second time.

How on earth could I have been such a major asshole to them? he wondered. *They didn't deserve any of the crap I dished out. But fuck... seeing them together was a kick to the nuts. Ivy is just as... no, even* more *beautiful than I remember, and the look she gave me when she latched onto his dick made me nearly come in my pants. That woman has* cojones *for miles.* He looked down to confirm that he was still as hard as he'd been witnessing their lovemaking—as if there were any doubt. *And holy Moses, Cooper is ripped. He's always looked good, but he's been working out more lately. And that huge schlong of his made me want to jump his bones too.* Bodhi shivered. *But where is this coming from? Why do I want to grab a fistful of Cooper's thick coppery hair and take a nip at his ass? It must have been the way he clenched his butt cheeks to get Ivy's grip on his dick moving. It raised him up into her hand, and she gripped him so tightly, the head turned a lovely shade of red.* Bodhi whipped off his boxers and grabbed his own shaft, then began to stroke it as he thought about what Cooper's would feel like in his fist. Then he pulled his hand away. *What am I doing?* he asked himself.

Bodhi was a master of telling himself the wrong things about his... urges. He was much more caught up in what he thought he *ought* to feel than what he truly felt. Hence, his stupid move to England to "further his career." He was doing great in that department right here at home and basically left because he was worried that he was getting too attached to Ivy when he wasn't ready for a forever relationship, and he was messed up in the head about Cooper. So, he told everyone it was an opportunity he couldn't pass up. *Yeah, sure.*

And then, his time in London turned into a nightmare and he couldn't get out of there fast enough.

Bodhi tossed around on the bed for a few more minutes, but his stiff dick was getting in the way of going to sleep, so he headed for the shower. The hot water relaxed him considerably—especially after he rubbed one out to the thoughts of Ivy and Cooper. He didn't know who turned him on more, but his orgasm crashed through him when he thought about Cooper's seed spurting all over them and the primal sound his buddy had made as he'd thrown his head back in ecstasy. The thing was, Bodhi couldn't decide if he wanted to feel Ivy's mouth on him that way or if he wanted to suck Cooper off the way she had. He wondered what it would taste like, and then he chastised himself for wondering.

Bodhi had no answers for himself, so he dried off and hit the bed again. This time he went to sleep and stayed there for about four hours.

* * *

When Bodhi finally woke up, he was ravenous, so he headed to the kitchen. Nearing his destination, he heard Ivy and Cooper having a discussion.

"I do not want to be forced to move out," he heard Cooper say in an angry tone. "I've invested a lot of money over the past year in this place and I like it."

"Well, how can we stay? He obviously owns the house and doesn't want us here. We can't live where we're not welcome. Maybe I'll just go camp out with a girlfriend until I can find my own place if you won't come with me."

Bodhi couldn't stand it. He was obviously driving a wedge between them, and things did not sound good. He loudly cleared his throat and entered the kitchen. "Uh... hi, guys. Is there any coffee?" he asked sheepishly.

Cooper pointed to the coffee maker and said, "Help yourself. Cream's in the fridge."

Apparently, Cooper remembered how he liked his java. *At least that was something positive*, Bodhi thought to himself. He grabbed a tall mug from the cupboard and poured himself a hot drink. Looking up and finding the two of them staring at him like he'd sprouted two heads, he sat down at the table with them and said, "Look, I'm really, really sorry about earlier. All I can say is, the flight was long and noisy, and I had the headache from hell. I got in early and showed up here, all relieved and shit to be home, but the sight of the two of you really threw me, you know?"

Neither answered, but Ivy narrowed her eyes at him.

"Okay, well, I owe you both an apology for what I said, and for... um... not leaving you two alone so you could... um..." He looked round as if there were clues stacked around the kitchen that would help him say what he meant. Since nothing popped out at him, he asked, "Is there anything to eat? I'm starving."

"There's some leftover takeout from last night," Ivy said with a suppressed chuckle. She knew Bodhi hated spicy Thai food, and that's all there was unless he wanted cold cereal, or he could break down and make himself a sandwich. She knew she wasn't about to offer to do it for him. She turned back to Cooper and said, "I think I'll go call Christy and then pack up my stuff. She has a nice, big couch in her apartment."

"No, Ivy. Please." Bodhi reached for her arm as she stalked past him and then he pulled back, thinking better of it before grabbing her. Instead, he said in a rush, "You don't have to leave. I was being an asshole, and I don't want you sleeping on some random sofa because I can't get my shit together. Apparently, I've missed a lot of what's been going on around here, and if you and Cooper are a... thing now, I'll have to accept it." He stood and rummaged through the refrigerator coming up with cream and some takeout cartons. He mumbled to himself, "I don't have to like it much, though." Opening the carton of spicy green curry, Bodhi grimaced and scooted the carton back onto the shelf, sighing, "Is there any peanut butter?"

Eventually, he made himself three peanut butter sandwiches and wolfed them down like he hadn't eaten in a week. Ivy and Cooper left him to dine alone. He knew he had a lot of making up and explaining to do. After his sandwiches and a couple tall coffees, he felt a lot more human, so he went in search of them.

Cooper and Ivy were sitting outside in the sun talking quietly. Both looked up when Bodhi slid the door open and plopped himself down in a free lawn chair. The sun sparkled off Ivy's shiny cascade of black hair and glinted in Cooper's almost-too-long-for-a-lawyer's reddish-brown waves. They were both tanned from California living—a fact that stood in sharp contrast to Bodhi's pallor. He appeared to have lost every bit of color. His hair was naturally a golden blond, but its sunny highlights had faded, and his skin appeared nearly translucent.

Ivy eyed him critically. Bodhi had always prided himself on his appearance. It was strange to see him looking so pale and drawn. He was like a shadow of his former self. It was a bit alarming, even though he was still an extremely handsome man. He'd lost his shine and dash, which didn't do him any good. This was enhanced by his hangdog expression, especially when he ran a hand over his face and sighed.

"Look, guys, I apologize again. Can we just start over and forget this morning ever happened?"

Instead of answering, Ivy asked, "Are you okay? You don't look very well."

"Yeah, I'm fine. I'm just exhausted, freaked out, and pissed off. Not at you guys," he hastened to say. "Things in London got kind of hairy, and I had to get out of there. I felt like any more of that rat race was going to kill me, you know?"

"I don't know. Care to explain?" answered Cooper in a flat voice with an edge to it. Apparently, he was less concerned than Ivy about Bodhi's appearance—or maybe he didn't notice things like that as readily.

Sighing, Bodhi explained, "London was a fiasco." He shook his head and looked away briefly. "The pace I had to keep was brutal. I worked from six in the morning until well after midnight every day for months and months. It was lucrative for me and my clients, yes, but I felt like I'd sold my soul to the devil to make all of that money. I was living on coffee to stay awake and getting only three or four hours of sleep each night —if I was lucky." No one commented, so he went on, "Finally, I saw that the office was taking shape and the other people were catching on about how to do things, so I took a few steps back and tried to be more social. I decided it was time to enjoy myself a little. That didn't go all that well either, but I made a few friends and got a little more sleep. Not much, though." He laughed ruefully to himself and did not elaborate. "Then stuff got weird for me, and I realized I needed to quit the job and head home. So, here I am. I don't have a job, but at least I have plenty of money to live on. More than enough, actually."

"Clear as mud," Ivy muttered. "So, now what? Are you going to find a new job? Sell this house? What?"

Bodhi looked into his mug of coffee and blew out his breath. "I don't know about working other than managing the investments I have. Maybe I'll take a breather while I figure that out. I have no plans to sell the house, and if you both want to stay, I'll take Cooper's old room. It's fine. I do need to buy a car pretty soon, though, since I doubt anyone is going to want to chauffeur me around."

Cooper squinted at Bodhi while Ivy snorted and muttered, "You got that part right." Then she looked him square in the eyes and asked, "So, are you a voyeur now?"

"Are you an exhibitionist?" Bodhi countered.

"I liked it," laughed Cooper.

They both stared at him.

"What? It's true. And don't try to deny that the two of you got off on it either."

Ivy's face went scarlet, and she self-consciously reached up to tuck a strand of hair behind her ear. As she did so, the sun glinted off her ring, and Bodhi's eyes suddenly went huge.

"What the hell is that on your finger, Ivy?" he rasped.

She held up her hand and looked at it as if she were seeing it for the first time as well. Her expression was unreadable.

Cooper broke the silence by announcing in a voice that was a little too loud, "I asked Ivy to marry me a few days ago, and she said yes." He had a huge smile on his face as he reached his hand toward Bodhi as if expecting his friend to shake it in congratulations.

Bodhi just stared at Ivy, then he silently stood, walked back into the house, and headed to his new bedroom. He didn't emerge again until the next morning. By then, Cooper had gone to work. Ivy was home because it was Monday, and her gallery was closed.

Bodhi found Ivy staring at her computer in the kitchen. She had coffee and a muffin sitting next to her laptop, but she seemed to be ignoring both. Bodhi poured himself a mug and located a fresh muffin for his breakfast before he sat down across from her. He took a healthy bite and exclaimed, "These are great. Did you bake them?"

"Uh-huh," she answered without looking at him.

"Ivy."

"Hmm?" Her eyes were still on the computer screen.

"I need to talk to you."

"So talk. No one's stopping you."

"Can you stop staring at nothing and look at me, please?"

She sighed and closed the laptop lid, raising her eyes to his with a cautious expression. "What?"

"I'll never be able to apologize enough for leaving you the way I did. It was cowardly and rude. I'm so sorry. You have no idea."

"Look, what's done is done. It hurt like hell, but I got over it," she lied. "You made your point by leaving, and I've moved on." She took a swallow of her coffee and started fiddling with the paper cup on her muffin.

Regarding her downcast eyes once again, Bodhi said, "Well, it wasn't honest, and I was a total fool."

Her eyes snapped to his. "What are you talking about?"

"I was too fixated on all of the wrong things to admit how much I was in love with you, and I wasn't even honest with myself." He heard Ivy give a small gasp as he continued, "I'll be sorry about that for the rest of my life." He reached toward her as if to grasp her hand, but she pulled away. "Are you happy with Cooper?"

"Yes. I am. I *trust* Cooper." Her eyes narrowed as she stared at him, mistrust evident on her face. "How convenient for you that you finally came to your senses when you know you're way too late. Don't go trying to undermine what I have with him, Bodhi. I know how controlling you can be. You stomped on my heart, and I sure don't want to go there again, so stay out of it."

"I missed you so much. You have no idea," he whispered.

"Are you delusional? Not one word of apology from you for a whole year, and you never even checked to see if I was alive! You can't mean what you're saying because you have no heart, Bodhi. None!" Her voice grew in volume and passion, and she seemed to be fighting tears. "Did someone dump you in London and that sent you packing? Did you want to come back to poor little Ivy who must be sitting around pining for her long-lost love or some crazy shit like that?" Her huge brown eyes seemed to be throwing daggers at him. "Did you get a taste of what it feels like to be abandoned and forgotten?"

"Hardly," he scoffed. "And I knew you were doing okay because Cooper mentioned you now and then when he'd text me."

"Big whoop."

"He sure as hell never mentioned that the two of you were shacking up. Only that he knew you were okay. Little did I know how well he knew it." Ivy eyed Bodhi suspiciously as his voice cracked with emotion. "I hope you're happy, I really do. Please don't hate me, though. I couldn't stand knowing that. You have to understand how quickly I came to my senses and... God, I missed you. I missed this place, I missed surfing, and I... uh... missed... Cooper. I left everything and everyone I love just because someone *flattered* me and told me I'd make a huge name for myself and make a ton of money by heading up the company in London when I could have had it all right here. I was so fucking stupid, Ivy!" He hung his head. "I'm ashamed of myself. I let blind ambition and fear of commitment wreck everything. They sent me over there knowing the office was actually in shambles and no one else wanted to go."

"Well… now what?" Ivy asked. "It's pretty weird living in the same house with you, especially after you just declared your love for me. And Cooper and I need our privacy, so…"

Bodhi's attention snapped to her. "Are you sure about that?" he broke in, cocking his head slightly.

"What do you mean by that?" Ivy asked, stiffening.

Bodhi finally gave her a shadow of a smile. "Well, I don't know. You seemed pretty happy to have me watch you blow Cooper, and he certainly got off on it. He even admitted he enjoyed it, so don't get all fake prim and proper about it now. I heard you cry out my name while you guys were having your fun too, so what was that all about?"

Turning beet red, Ivy looked away. "Don't get the wrong idea. It wasn't what it may have sounded like."

Bodhi remembered the laughter that followed her cry and decided maybe he would be happier not knowing, but he couldn't make himself let it alone. "No? So, what was it, huh? You wanted me to come back and play? You missed me?"

"Drop it, Bodhi. You won't like the answer."

"Right. Well, we can possibly agree to disagree on that one, but it sounded pretty sexy to me, and I don't mind saying I wouldn't be opposed to joining in on some of your fun—if that's what you want."

"What are you suggesting?" Ivy squirmed a little in her seat and continued to blush.

"Are you attracted to me, Ivy? The truth."

She frowned and answered, "You're still… attractive to me, even though you're as pale as the Pillsbury Doughboy now. But physical attraction doesn't mean I want to follow through on anything with you."

Throwing back his head, Bodhi laughed. "That's what a year in London and away from the beach will do to you. I've lost my Golden Boy glow—is that what you're saying?"

"Yeah," she laughed softly. "You look a little pasty."

"A few days in the sun will restore my previous vitality," he said with a smirk. "And then how will you be able to resist me?"

"Bodhi! I'm ashamed of you. I'm engaged to Cooper, and I'm not going to cheat on him, tan or no tan. That's just stupid talk."

"We'll see." Privately he thought she was a hundred percent right, and he wouldn't butt in, but it was fun to jab at her.

"No, we sure as hell won't see, Bodhi Monaghan!"

Her eyes flashed at him angrily and he felt himself getting hard. He'd always loved to rile her up a little because the sex was incredible when she was emotional. He chuckled at her.

Changing the subject, Ivy asked, "Why don't you ask Cooper when he'll be home this evening, and maybe the two of you can go surf for an hour or so?"

"Excellent idea, my beautiful Ivy."

"I'm *not* yours."

"Go on telling yourself that if it makes you happy."

"God, you're insufferably conceited!"

"I know." Bodhi shoved the remaining bite of muffin into his mouth and smiled at her. "Mmm," he moaned.

Chapter Seven

Later that evening, the two men grabbed their boards and headed down to the beach. They didn't return until well after the sun had set, and both of them looked pleased with themselves. In typical guy fashion, they seemed to be relaxing around each other by just spending time together and not talking about anything but their shared enjoyment of surfing. When they got back to the house, Ivy was waiting. Cooper and Bodhi hurried off to take showers before dinner. When they returned, Ivy was piling the last of the tacos onto a large platter.

"How was it?" Ivy asked.

"Great," exclaimed Bodhi as Cooper reached into the refrigerator to grab some beers. "Thank you for fixing dinner, Ivy. You didn't have to do that for us."

She shrugged noncommittally. "Eh, we have to eat, and I was in a taco mood. There's mild salsa in this bowl and real salsa in the blue one."

Cooper snorted something that sounded like "Wuss."

Bodhi ignored Cooper's jab at his dislike for hot food and sat down at the table. He reached for a taco and began adding his favorite toppings to it along with mild salsa. It touched him that Ivy had thought to provide it for him. Somehow this indicated to him that she still cared for him deep down. At least she was paying attention.

They made polite small talk about surfing and Ivy's gallery throughout the meal, not touching on anything that might disrupt their tentative harmony.

After dinner was over, Cooper and Ivy snuggled together at one end of the couch to watch a movie, leaving Bodhi a spot at the other end. He positioned himself halfway between the arm of the sofa and the couple—within reach if he wanted to touch Ivy. They seemed to ignore his proximity.

The movie was boring as all get-out, but there was a fairly exciting bedroom scene in the middle of it that seemed to give Cooper some ideas. He started kissing Ivy—slowly at first, but gradually with more and more ardor. His hand slid up and he pulled down the neck of her tank top, exposing her lovely breasts. He stroked and fondled her, playing with her nipples as she moaned encouragingly.

As if magnetized, Bodhi scooted a little bit closer and caught Cooper's eye. Cooper didn't look at all displeased with Bodhi and took that opportunity to remove his hand from Ivy's boob, only to undo her pants and slide it between her legs. She let out a gasp of pleasure. He subtly cocked one eyebrow at Bodhi as if in challenge. Of what, Bodhi wasn't certain.

Does he want to drive me crazy? Does he want me to join in? Should I leave the room? Bodhi's hands itched to touch Ivy— and Cooper, but he dared not try it without a direct invitation. He wished fervently he had the gumption to get up and leave, but he was anchored in place.

Cooper kept kissing and playing with Ivy until she stiffened in his arms and let out a sound that Bodhi knew all too well— the sound she made when she had a satisfying orgasm.

Bodhi's dick was so hard watching this display, he thought he was going to rip a hole in his sweatpants. He ached to touch himself—or touch one of them. Finally, deciding they were toying with him, and he couldn't take it any longer, he stood abruptly and stalked out of the room. He needed to take care of business before he made a mess of himself. He headed for the main bathroom in the hall and rubbed one out. It took less than two minutes, and he tried valiantly to be quiet about it, only to let out a colossal groan when he came. He imagined them laughing at him and wished he could be less obvious.

However, after cleaning himself up, he exited the bathroom and looked back down the hall. He caught sight of Cooper's bare ass as he pounded rhythmically into Ivy—right there on the couch. *My couch,* he thought. He was sure they were going to make a mess of it, so without thinking of the consequences, he stormed back toward them. As he got closer, Ivy's sleek legs wrapped themselves around Cooper and she cried out, "Harder! I need it rough tonight!"

As if spellbound, Bodhi watched Cooper's beautiful glutes contract and relax with each mighty pump. Bodhi's feet took over for his brain and propelled him closer and closer, and... holy crap, he was hard again already!

In the dim light from the television, Bodhi caught sight of Ivy's facial expression. She appeared to be transported into sheer bliss, but then slowly she opened her eyes and locked them onto Bodhi's gaze. A small smile appeared, and then her eyes seemed to roll back as she closed them again. Obviously, she was aware of his presence in the room with them, and it hadn't dulled her enjoyment one whit.

Not knowing what to do despite his longing, Bodhi stood rooted to the spot as he'd done when he'd caught them before.

Soon, Cooper's pace became erratic and nearly brutal as he pounded his way toward release. He cried out, roaring with ecstasy.

Bodhi felt light-headed as he watched his friend come inside the woman he still loved. With a mixture of pain, regret, excitement, and profound longing, he stood on wobbly legs and stared as Cooper pulled out. It was then that he caught a glimpse of Ivy's glistening pussy. Cooper stood and said, "Be right back." He planted a quick kiss on Ivy's mouth.

Seeing that Cooper was leaving to get rid of his condom, Bodhi's sense of fastidiousness was comforted. They hadn't made a mess after all—not that he had actually remembered his earlier worry. He fixated instead on Cooper's giant shlong that was growing soft as he sauntered past and headed down the hall. As Cooper disappeared into the bathroom, Bodhi's attention went back to Ivy who was still spraddled somewhat open-legged right in front of him.

"Obviously you liked what you saw, didn't you, Bodhi?" she asked sitting up. "We could hear you through the door. Too bad you lost the right to play with this." She gestured to her body as she snatched up her clothing and began putting it back on.

Cooper reemerged just then. "How badly do you want to touch her right now, Bodhi?" he asked with a smirk. Then he did something that shocked the shit out of Bodhi. Cooper walked right up to him and pressed his naked body against Bodhi's back, reaching around and pressing Bodhi into him. He breathed into Bodhi's ear, "You'd like to eat her out right now, wouldn't you?"

Bodhi could feel every one of Cooper's muscles against his back through his soft t-shirt, and he blushed at the feel of Cooper pushing his junk into his ass crack. With a mighty shrug of his shoulders, he escaped Cooper's grip and bolted from the room. He might want them both, but he was sure this was just a mean game of nasty retaliation on their part for his desertion. Also, his conscience told him over and over that Ivy was an engaged woman and he needed to stay away.

Chapter Eight

Over the next week, Bodhi's torture continued.

Unbeknownst to Bodhi, Ivy had several conversations with Cooper about how to continue their games with Bodhi. She loved the idea of being with the two of them, but she was still angry enough with Bodhi to want to torture him a bit more.

"Shouldn't we just ask him to come to bed with us?" Cooper asked. He favored a straightforward approach.

"We could," she mused. "But I want him to suffer a little," she said with a mischievous smile. "I think we should tease him and see how long it'll take him to show up on his own. Care to place a wager on how long it might take him to cave in?"

"Hah! No. He'll show up when his balls are blue enough if you keep flaunting this sweet body of yours," Cooper whispered as he nuzzled her neck and caressed her breast.

Chuckling softly, Ivy answered, "I have a strong feeling he's just as hot for you."

* * *

Ivy usually removed her business attire as soon as she got back from work—replacing it with a skimpy pair of shorts and a tight tank top with no bra. It just about killed Bodhi to see her perky nipples poking through the thin material. She had the most perfect tits he'd ever seen, and the desire to touch them and taste them was driving him nuts.

Since the house wasn't air-conditioned—as was common in the area homes—Cooper seemed to think most clothing was optional as well and usually walked around in shorts, but never with a shirt on. Bodhi tried not to stare and lust after either of his housemates. Unfortunately for him, it was a struggle.

Bodhi tried to put his housemates out of his mind while they were at work, but it was nearly impossible. He took his laptop outside to sit in the warm sun and attempted to immerse himself in managing his investments. When he needed a break, he researched what car to buy. However, all too often he found himself staring at the screen with no idea what he was doing—his mind drifting to the scene that played out in front of him on movie night. He burned to relive that experience. He just didn't want to have them laugh at him and boot him out. He was certain this was some kind of test.

His personal mantra became *Stay away. They're engaged.*

* * *

Every day, Bodhi's phone would ring with a familiar number, and he ignored each call with a disgusted look on his face. Eventually, as the calls increased in frequency and grew closer and closer together, he blocked the number. He'd had it with the caller and couldn't be bothered with any more drama.

The only time Bodhi felt at ease was when he and Cooper hit the beach with their boards. The roaring surf drowned out his audio memory of Ivy's ecstatic cries down the hall at night. And the cold water shriveled his semi-hard dick back into a semblance of control. Cooper's body was safely encased in a wetsuit, so Bodhi wasn't tempted by seeing his toned and golden physique on display. He just watched the waves and selected wisely each time he wanted to ride one to shore. It was a great feeling that he'd missed terribly. When the surf was up like this, he had a hard time reconciling his burning need to escape to London a year ago. He'd been such an idiot.

* * *

After several agonizing episodes of telling himself to stay put while he could hear them in bed together, Bodhi couldn't resist the temptation any longer. Late on Saturday night, he heard unmistakable murmurs coming from his old bedroom and suddenly felt compelled to check out the action. He crept down the hall on silent bare feet and slowly positioned himself so that he could see through the open doorway. He didn't fool anyone for even a second.

As soon as his face appeared in the opening, Ivy exclaimed, "Oh look, he's finally here." Her face bore an enigmatic expression.

Cooper raised his face up from where he'd been teasing Ivy's breasts with his mouth and chuckled. "Are you ready?" he asked.

Bodhi's dick pulsed in his pajama bottoms, and he felt lightheaded. As he admired their beautiful naked bodies in the moonlight, he cleared his throat. "Ready for what, exactly?"

"Ready to watch again. You seemed to like it so much. And I know Ivy and I did."

Bodhi's feet once again propelled him almost involuntarily into the room where he plunked himself down on the foot of the bed. "What are you two playing at? Are you trying to make me nuts? I can't stop thinking about the two of you, and it's driving me *insane*." He looked at their smug faces as he dragged his hand roughly through his hair. "Is this how you want to pay me back for deserting you? If so... well done, my friends, I am officially ruined."

Ivy spoke up—ignoring his question. "I wouldn't say you're off the hook exactly, but if you want to play, we're up for some fun."

"Play. What do you mean?" Bodhi felt his face burning, but he couldn't make himself get up and leave. "Do you want me to pretend I'm a chastened cuckold? Jealous lover? What?"

"Whatever floats your boat," chuckled Cooper. "We just know the sex is hotter when you're here. Call us selfish if you like, but you showed up here on your own volition, so..."

"Can I touch?" Bodhi blurted out in a strangled voice.

Cooper and Ivy stared at each other for a moment, and a private conversation seemed to pass between them as they spoke with their eyes. Ivy gave a sly smile and looked at Bodhi finally. She answered softly with a small shrug, "You can try it and see how I like it."

Bodhi's eyes narrowed as he contemplated how everything apparently had to be on *their* terms. *I'll just have to be inventive*, he decided. Anyway, his dick was so hard he thought he'd explode any moment, and he needed some relief. Instead of commenting further, he stood and slid off his flannel pants. "I'm probably going to go to hell for this," he muttered softly to himself.

Cooper swiveled Ivy into position and had her face Bodhi as he pulled her atop his erection in reverse cowgirl position. Speaking softly into Ivy's ear, he explained, "Bodhi can see all of the action this way. I bet he'd love to watch your beautiful tits bounce while you fuck." He then raised her up and slid her down onto his dick.

Ivy's eyes closed and her chest heaved. "Ohh, baby. You fill me up so well. I've never had such a perfect dick inside me," she crooned as she slowly worked his length into her. "Mmm. Feels *so* good. And I love it with no condom this time."

Ignoring what may have been a cruel—and unwarranted—cock comparison, Bodhi crawled over and grabbed Cooper's ankles, shoving them apart to make room for himself as he knelt between his buddy's legs. He bent down to get a good view of where they were joined and locked his eyes onto where Cooper appeared and disappeared inside Ivy as she rose and fell. Everything glistened with her juices, and Bodhi was dying to sample a taste.

He started by touching her with a butterfly soft caress, swirling his finger around where she was the most sensitive. She gave the tiniest of jolts when she felt him, but didn't shrink away, so his touch became bolder. He zeroed in on her clit and began rubbing it rhythmically. Ivy began to writhe under his touch, so he pushed against her with more and more force, constantly rubbing and caressing her. Finally, as though he were a moth drawn to a flame, his need to taste overpowered him and Bodhi leaned in closer to lick Ivy. She let out a keening moan that startled him, but when he pulled back, she cried, "No, don't stop!"

Never one to disobey a direct order from a lady in the throes of passion, Bodhi bowed back down and began probing her in earnest with his tongue. He added his fingers, playing around her opening where she met up with Cooper's shaft. Then he sucked her clit deeply into his mouth and listened to her strangled cry. He sucked and probed her over and over with his lips and firm tongue, aware of a new sensation he'd never experienced before. As he licked and played with Ivy, sometimes holding her hard little bud gently in his teeth as he thrashed it with his tongue, his chin and fingers kept rubbing against Cooper. Bodhi went so far as to adjust his angle so that he could feel more of Cooper that way. He wondered what his scruff felt like against the base of Cooper's erection. *Does it tickle? Scrape? Feel as hot to Cooper as it does to me?* Lost in these multiple thoughts and still maintaining firm pressure on Ivy's clit, he wasn't ready to stop when Ivy cried out, shaking with her orgasm.

Upon hearing her cries, Bodhi's brain shut off. Instinct took over as he grabbed Cooper's shaft with one hand and pulled it out of Ivy. He roughly shoved three fingers into her and pumped in and out while he held tightly onto Cooper... and engulfed Cooper's dick in his mouth.

Cooper hollered, "What the *fuck*, Bodhi?" But his exclamation quickly morphed into a long groan as Bodhi ignored his question and kept sucking.

Ivy's eyes popped open, and she stared down at the sight in front of her.

Still manipulating Ivy with one hand, Bodhi felt like a one-man-band. His other hand pumped up and down on Cooper's shaft as he sucked his friend for all he was worth. Ivy seemed to be coming again, or maybe she was still shaking from her last orgasm—it was hard to tell.

When Ivy's shuddering subsided, Bodhi yanked his fingers out of her and grabbed his own throbbing hard-on, squeezing and pumping himself for all he was worth. His hand was slick with her juices, allowing him to slide with ease.

Cooper was moaning his head off, and Bodhi felt like the sexiest man alive. He loved the power and control he had over them. *They thought they could manipulate the situation. Hah!* he thought to himself. And then he felt the first spurt of Cooper's jizz pouring into his mouth. *Hmm. That's an interesting taste. Not bad. Just new.* He sucked even harder and squeezed Cooper who was hollering and swearing—but it sounded like surprised ecstasy rather than anger.

Bodhi swallowed a few times and relaxed his hand on Cooper. He gave himself a couple more pumps and, with a satisfied roar, came all over his hand.

After a few silent seconds, he stood and headed into the bathroom for a quick clean-up. On his way back out, he looked at their startled faces. Bodhi smiled smugly and said, "You're welcome." Snatching his pajamas up from the floor, he strode from the room.

Back in his own bed, Bodhi had a lot to think about, and all of it was... amazing.

Chapter Nine

Sunday morning, Cooper didn't seem to be able to make eye contact with Bodhi.

Bodhi, on the other hand, was more chipper than he'd been in years.

They'd found him in the kitchen with a fresh pot of coffee brewing and the ingredients for some pretty snazzy-looking omelets all chopped and ready to go. There was fresh orange juice on the table and a plate of Ivy's muffins in the middle.

"I worked up quite an appetite last night," he explained matter-of-factly. "I hope you two got a good night's sleep. Omelet, anyone?" He stood before them poised with a pan in one hand and an egg in the other.

"Uh, sure. Thanks," Ivy answered.

"Yeah, okay," Cooper grumbled as he went to pour a couple mugs of coffee.

Turning out a perfect omelet, he divided it onto a couple of plates that he set in front of them. Then Bodhi announced, "Last night was great." He regarded Cooper's scarlet face and added, "No need to be embarrassed. It was your idea, you know."

"Not you suck... not what you did to me! That wasn't my idea," Cooper spluttered.

"Chill, bro. I'm not going to call the sex police on you. You had some fun, so embrace it and get over it." Bodhi looked at Ivy who studied her omelet like it might talk to her any minute. "Ivy liked it, didn't you, honey?"

Ivy grabbed a lock of hair and twirled it absently. In a small voice she admitted, "Yes." Then she looked at Cooper and added, "It was kind of amazing."

Cooper's face twisted. "The watching or the guy-on-guy shit?"

In a stronger voice she answered, "I loved watching Bodhi suck you off. I've never seen anything like that before."

There, she admitted it, Bodhi thought. He grinned victoriously as she continued.

"I'd like to see more of it actually. Could you do it to Bodhi?"

"Jeezus!" Cooper hollered. He stood and marched out of the room as he heard Bodhi snickering behind him.

"Boners don't lie, Cooper," he called out. "You planning on taking care of that? I'll be glad to come help." Laughing, he turned to Ivy. "Our boy there seems to be a little turned on right now, and he doesn't want to admit it."

Ivy snorted and tried to look serious. It wasn't working.

"I have a question for you, though, Ivy. You guys were using a condom when I saw you in the living room, and now you're not. What gives?"

Ivy blushed and answered softly, "We used one that time because Cooper was afraid of making a mess on what he called 'your precious couch.' I'm on the pill though, so once he was tested, we quit using them for birth control."

Nodding as though this all made good sense to him, Bodhi said, "Well, just so you know, I'm clean—in case you're wondering." He winked and grabbed the omelet he'd set in front of Cooper and set to downing it himself. "I'll make him another one as soon as he's done *jacking off*. It's a shame to waste hot food." He'd raised his voice on the words "jacking off" so Cooper could hear him from down the hall.

* * *

I should hate this, Cooper thought to himself. But, try as he might, he couldn't deny the feelings he had. He'd often had to pull his eyes off Bodhi's physique back when they played beach volleyball together. The memory of all of Bodhi's golden charm was etched in Cooper's memory. The strong, well-defined muscles, the tanned, smooth skin. It was all beautiful. But Bodhi's face looked to Cooper like a fallen angel with those mischievous hazel eyes and his thick mop of blond hair. He had the most perfect dimple in his chin, and Cooper had wanted to touch it on more than one occasion. He remembered how Bodhi's powerful legs would propel him into the air to spike a ball that Cooper had set up for him. And he remembered what Bodhi's body looked like all stretched out reaching and leaping to make the spike. He was a sculpted work of art with his shorts riding low on his hips and his tanned abs and biceps stretching and flexing in the sunlight.

He thought of how, when they were done playing ball on the beach and hit the water, Bodhi would whoop with joy when he caught the perfect wave.

It all came crashing in on Cooper finally. He'd missed Bodhi as much or more than Ivy had.

He wanted to punish Bodhi for deserting him. Or rather them... deserting *them*. That's what he *meant* to think.

He wanted Bodhi.

He didn't want to want Bodhi.

Why did Bodhi have to come back and get in the middle of what I have with Ivy? It would have been so easy to just marry her and get on with our lives.

Cooper decided he needed to get out of the house to think for a while, so he put on his board shorts and headed for the garage with the intent of going to the beach. He was loading his longboard onto the rack on his car when Bodhi appeared.

"Heading out?" he asked. When Cooper nodded without comment, he added, "Want some company?"

Cooper glared at Bodhi for a moment and then said, "Not really."

"Well, I brought you some toast. I thought you ought to eat something before you leave," Bodhi explained as he stretched out his hand holding the food. "You shouldn't go surfing by yourself *or* on an empty stomach."

Narrowing his eyes, Cooper asked, "Since when do you care what I do, Bodhi?" He took the toast, however, and stuffed a piece in his mouth.

"I always care. You're my *best friend*, Cooper. And I'm sorry if what I did bothered you so much last night. I hope it hasn't ruined our friendship because I think that would be a terrible thing." Bodhi looked away and then back again saying softly, "I'm really sorry man. I guess I misread the signals on purpose because I told myself you wanted it. I don't know what came over me. It just... I just... felt compelled to do it."

"You don't have to do anything like that because you feel sorry for me, Bodhi!" Cooper nearly shouted.

Bodhi's head jerked back like he'd been slapped. "Sorry for you? Why should I feel sorry for you? You're engaged to Ivy, you're successful, smart, and a handsome stud. Yeah, my heart bleeds! What are you talking about?"

Cooper's face went scarlet, and he looked down at his feet. The second forgotten piece of toast dangled from his grasp. Then he took a deep breath and skewered Bodhi with a laser glare. "I assumed you'd noticed me looking at you over the years and you felt like humoring me finally."

"Looking at me?"

"Yes, Bodhi. *Looking* at you. In case you haven't figured it out, I'm impossibly, hopelessly attracted to you and I fucking *loved* what you did last night. I don't know what this means because I've never been turned on by a guy before in my whole life. I mean, it was one thing to have you watching us fuck, and that was as hot as hell, but when you... did what you did? Shit, man, I can't believe what that did to me." Cooper reached up and grabbed a handful of his hair, looking lost. "I never thought of myself as bi, but that was incredible. I still get one hundred percent turned on by Ivy, but... well... fuck!"

Bodhi's expression went from concern to mild amusement to lust-filled as Cooper continued his rant.

"... But if that was some kind of consolation suck, then leave me alone from now on," Cooper ordered. "I don't need it."

Bodhi took a step closer to Cooper and stared into his eyes. Softly, he answered, "I did it because I wanted to, Coop. Not because I felt sorry for you or wanted to lead you on or anything like that. I saw what I wanted and I took it without asking. And I loved it too." He stepped closer once more. "I thought you and Ivy were trying to pay me back by tormenting me. I know you're mad that I left you guys, and I'm sorrier than you'll ever know about that. But to answer your question about noticing you looking at me—no. I wasn't aware of it because I was probably trying to be so sly about watching you, and it never occurred to me that the feeling was reciprocated. I don't know how to flirt with a guy, for Chrissake. I've never done it in my life. I've never even wanted to before. Maybe I came on a little strong for the first time, though." He snickered.

"Yeah, well... you really did go in for the kill," Cooper said with a laugh. "So, what are we saying here? We're suddenly gay or something?"

Bodhi laughed. "I don't think that it's all that sudden, and I think it's definitely more bi than gay, but I'm sick of pretending it's not there—especially if you feel it too." He reached up and stroked his hand along Cooper's jaw and into his hair.

Cooper's eyes closed and he turned his face into Bodhi's hand like a cat that craved his touch. "So now what?" He opened his eyes with a start. "What about Ivy?"

Bodhi left his hand in place, saying, "What about her? She seemed pretty turned on by us. You heard her just a little while ago—she wanted more of what we did. Or... what I did." He let that register for a moment. "Why don't we go talk to her about it... unless you have your heart set on surfing this morning."

"Nah, not really. The waves are flat today according to the surf report. I was more interested in getting out and clearing my head." Closing the gap between their bodies, Cooper felt Bodhi's warmth spread through him. He stared into Bodhi's hazel eyes and said, "I'm still really, really pissed at you for leaving, but at least it got Ivy and me together. She's my fiancée, Bodhi, so don't forget it."

"Why do you think I've been such a mental case? I understand you're engaged, and it hurts like a motherfucker, but I don't want to mess up your lives. I just can't stop wanting both of you and I never stopped loving either of you, no matter how far away I was."

Cooper sucked in a startled breath.

"Yeah, Cooper. I said it. I've been in love with you just as much as I'm in love with Ivy, only for a much longer time."

This time it was Cooper's hand that reached for Bodhi's face and pulled him closer. Their mouths crashed together in a searing kiss born of want and desire. They kissed like they were battling for supremacy. Nothing gentle happened there. It was a kiss made of teeth clashing, lip-biting, tongue-sucking, and primal growls. It went on and on as they tasted each other, nipped at each other, all the while grinding their hard bodies together with hungry, rutting confusion.

It may have been seconds or minutes or hours—they both lost all track of time, but they pulled away when a startled gasp came from the side door of the garage. Ivy had come looking for them. "Oh! I... um... just came out to see if you'd both left for the beach, but I never heard a car leave. Sorry to... um... disturb you." She started to back away but then she paused and studied the two of them. "But... so... what's going on, guys?"

Cooper looked embarrassed and pulled his hands away from Bodhi's body as Bodhi turned to Ivy. "I was just explaining to Cooper what the Brits call snogging—a new word I learned in London. He says it's tonsil hockey, and I think he wins because he scored." Bodhi looked at Cooper's red face and chuckled, then he acknowledged Ivy's equally red visage and announced, "Relax, everyone. Cooper and I finally admitted our attraction to each other, and I went a step further and let him know how much I still love both of you. What you just saw was the result of that confession. Cool, huh?"

Ivy's eyes bugged and her jaw dropped. Then she started to leak tears as she pulled off her engagement ring and thrust it into Cooper's hand. "I'll go call my friend and be out of your way." She turned to leave, but two strong hands grasped her arms—one from each guy.

"Don't go," Cooper said in a pleading voice at the same time Bodhi laughed and told her, "No reason to go anywhere, Ivy. I don't want to break you guys up. I wouldn't mind enhancing your relationship now and then with a little triple-time action, though." He wiggled his eyebrows at her startled face and then grew serious. "I meant what I said though. I still love you. I love Cooper too, and I was too much of a chickenshit to admit it to either of you. I messed up everything, and I can't tell you enough times how sorry I am."

Ivy looked at her feet and then back at the two men regarding her avidly. Letting out a huff of air, she said, "I think we all need to talk about this, so let's get out of this garage and go get comfortable somewhere, okay?"

"Bed?" asked Bodhi.

She narrowed her eyes at him. "Maybe eventually, but we need to have an adult conversation first, horndog."

"That sounds promising," Bodhi laughed. "Let's go."

Cooper still looked embarrassed as he followed Ivy back into the house. Bodhi was right on his heels.

Chapter Ten

After assessing the various places where they could get comfortable, they ended up sitting outside. The sunny patio had cushioned chairs that faced each other in a conversational grouping. It somehow seemed important that they sit alone for this chat rather than piled together in bed or on the couch where touching would distract them.

As soon as they were seated, Bodhi asked, "Ivy, do you still have *any* feelings for me? I know I messed up horribly, but sometimes love isn't all that easy to erase."

She looked at him thoughtfully before she answered. "You trashed my heart, Bodhi. It hurt so badly to give my love to someone who acted as callously as you did. That said... maybe I do have some lingering feelings for you. But I don't completely trust you. I honestly don't know if I could ever love you again the way that I did."

He nodded sadly. "I get it. I'm so sorry. You have no idea how badly I've regretted my actions."

Ivy looked at Cooper, who appeared crestfallen and added, "I'm sorry, Cooper. I hope it doesn't hurt your feelings that I haven't given up on Bodhi completely. It doesn't diminish my love for you one iota."

Cooper blew out a breath. "It's something I'll have to get used to. I can't sit here and say I love two people at the same time, but you're only allowed to love me. I can't be that selfish."

Bodhi's eyes lit up as he asked, "Are you saying you have feelings for me, Coop?"

Cooper blushed and stared at his hands for a beat. "I guess that's true. I've tried to suppress them for so long, it seems odd to finally voice my feelings, but I can't deny that I have a deep desire and... affection for you, Bodhi. I tried to stay so strong when you left because I was trying to help Ivy through her feelings of abandonment, so I barely acknowledged my own emotions through it all." He breathed in and bolstered himself before he said, "Yes. I love you as much as I love Ivy. I have for a long time."

Bodhi's jaw dropped for a second before he gave a fist pump and whispered victoriously, "Yes!"

"That doesn't mean I'm completely done being pissed off at you, though," Cooper added with a wry smile.

Everyone took turns speaking their mind after that, and Ivy became aware of both men's wishes to pursue a sexual experience with each other without excluding her. Their desires came out haltingly and tentative at first, but finally Bodhi spelled it out. Both men watched her closely, as if waiting for her to burst into tears. But in truth, the idea of Bodhi and Cooper together was so arousing to her, Ivy discovered she was on board with it completely.

Ivy pressed her lips together and leaned forward, looking back and forth between the two men. "Okay," she said at last.

"Okay?" Cooper repeated. "Ivy, is that... Does that mean...?"

Ivy nodded. "I'm up for it, if you guys are. I can see how it might work for us."

Cooper reached out tentatively and slid her engagement ring back onto her finger. They smiled at each other for a moment.

Ivy let out a little sigh. "I have a friend— a gallery customer —who comes in whenever I get a new exhibit. He's in a triad relationship. You might have heard of them—they live in La

Jolla. The famous romance writer and her two men? The guy I know is Casey Melrose. He's the nicest guy and, even though their private business was plastered all over the internet by some lunatic, he always seems so happy."

"Who wouldn't be ecstatic in that situation?" asked Bodhi with a wicked grin. "He has his cake, and he can eat anyone he wants... or however that saying goes."

Cooper finally laughed. He seemed to be relaxing now that the ring was back on Ivy's hand.

Wiping the smirk from his face finally, Bodhi implored them, "Let me in, you guys. For real. I want to be a part of you. I love you both, and I promise I'll do everything to earn your trust. I've been the biggest fool on earth to deny my emotions for so long, but now I..." his voice cracked, "need you."

Ivy looked skeptical and asked, "Just what changed for you all of a sudden? One minute you're a hotshot financial wizard in London, and the next you're showing up here out of the blue with no job. What happened?"

Breaking eye contact, Bodhi got a faraway look on his face before he answered quietly, "I realized, as I said before, that the pace I was keeping at work was about to kill me, and my social life was a wreck. I just had to get out of there. I missed everything and everyone."

"Care to be a little clearer so that those of us who weren't there can understand better?" Ivy asked.

"Not really. It's not a pleasant story." He looked at Ivy and then at Cooper and said, "I'm just really happy to be back here with you two. I can't express that enough."

"I have one more question for you, Bodhi. You contacted Cooper from time to time, but if you supposedly missed me so much and felt so awful about leaving, why didn't you ever..." her voice cracked, "get in touch with me?"

Bodhi's eyes were pools of regret when he answered, "I was afraid I'd lost the privilege, and..." he looked down and then back up at her, "quite honestly I was scared to death to hear how much you hated me."

She nodded thoughtfully and tried to not look *too* sympathetic. He'd dumped her pretty unceremoniously, after all. No one said anything for a while.

This was apparently as much of an answer as Bodhi was going to give them, so Cooper looked at Ivy and they had another one of their silent eyeballs-only conversations. After a moment, they both smiled, and Cooper announced, "I guess as long as you agree to take it slowly and don't go trying to break Ivy and me up so you can horn in on her by yourself, we can try it."

Bodhi let out a whoop, and Ivy seemed to give a weird little shudder as she clamped her legs together. "Ohmygawd," she whispered. "For real, I just had a mental orgasm just thinking about the possibilities." She fanned her face and burst out laughing. "I always thought that a touch-free orgasm was just a unicorn or bullshit, but... um... wow. That was fun." She immediately sobered, however, and leveled a no-nonsense look at Bodhi, saying, "You just better not ditch us again for no good reason. If you try that, it's the end. There will be no third chance. Got it?"

"Got it," he declared, raising his hand as if he were in court swearing to tell the truth and nothing but the truth. He placed his other hand over his heart.

* * *

Not being able to resist temptation, they headed for the big bed in the master bedroom and got naked. Each of them thought they'd positively died and gone to heaven as they experienced new sensations that could only come from having an extra pair of hands, an extra mouth, two gorgeous, virile penises instead of one, and the most receptive, responsive woman they could imagine. They kept things light for now, however.

The first thing they tried—encouraged by Ivy—was that the two men needed to learn how to touch each other. They'd kissed, and there was Bodhi's initial impromptu blowjob, but she thought they needed to master the art of foreplay a little before getting into the heavy stuff. "Feel each other," she urged them. "Cooper, use your hands on Bodhi. Feel his skin, his muscles, and when you're ready, touch his cock."

So Cooper did just that, going perhaps a little more quickly than Ivy had expected. He lunged for Bodhi's body as though starving for him and rubbed his face into Bodhi's chest as he grabbed for the erection that stood so large and proud between them. Bodhi moaned with the feel of Cooper's firm grip on his shaft and grabbed for Cooper the same way. Soon they moved in even closer, and both men's hands grasped their cocks together as one. They let out matching moans while their dicks rubbed against each other as they massaged them.

"Oh, so good," Bodhi sighed happily. He looked at Ivy for a second and realized she'd gotten so turned on she was energetically diddling her clit.

She gave him a sheepish grin and said, "This is a thousand times better than watching porn."

He leaned over and dragged her to him with his free hand. He kissed Ivy for the first time in over a year. *How odd*, he mused, *that this time I'm kissing her while playing with Cooper's dick simultaneously.* It made him feel like the luckiest man on earth. He still couldn't believe it.

The men then wanted to "double team" Ivy, as they called it. So, while Cooper feasted on and played with her tits, Bodhi went down on her. She lay in a writhing mess, overcome with the sensation of mouths and fingers all over the most sensitive areas of her body. Everywhere, it seemed, there were teasing lips and nipping teeth, tongues, and caressing fingers. She was stroked, petted, probed, savored, and held. All of the sensations built and built to a crescendo of ecstasy.

As they collapsed in the bed, Ivy panted, "I'm having a little bit of an emotional overload here, guys. I think we need to slow down a while." So, later that night when they went to bed, there was a lot of cuddling and kissing, but that's as far as it went. No one wanted to do too much too quickly and spoil their fun.

Over the next several days, Bodhi spent more and more time in the master bedroom with them and gradually moved his stuff into the closet. It was a bit of a squeeze, and it was becoming a little difficult to locate their things. Finally, they all decided to shift their belongings around to make use of the closet space so that the stuff they wanted most was in the master bedroom and the rest was in what they'd mostly stopped calling "Bodhi's room."

One thing was certain to each of them. This new arrangement was going to be a lot of fun.

Chapter Eleven

The morning of their first full weekend together, there was more kissing and fondling, but still no one seemed to be in a big hurry to push the envelope. They were still navigating the emotional elements of a triad.

For the most part, things seemed to be going smoothly, but from time to time, Cooper worried that Ivy was becoming too hung up on Bodhi and was ignoring him. He had to bury that thinking, he told himself. It was counterproductive and probably was his imagination. But... Bodhi was just so charismatic...

Just give it time, became his mantra. *She's still wearing your ring.* He couldn't ignore his own feelings for Bodhi, either, and the hypocrisy of his thoughts wasn't lost on him.

* * *

Ivy's stomach started growling, and the men laughingly decided she needed breakfast. As they were getting dressed, Bodhi suddenly remembered something.

"Oh hey, my new car is ready today, and I need to go pick it up from the dealer. Could one of you maybe give me a ride, or should I get an Uber?"

"I have some gallery work I need to do online, so why don't you guys go?" Ivy suggested. "I'm sure you're eager to get your wheels, and I might slow you down."

So, after making a big mess in the kitchen and eating a monstrous meal, the two men took off. Ivy surveyed the disarray and told herself to just deal with it. Bodhi was normally the neat freak of the two guys, but he'd been so anxious to get going, they'd left in a rush of good-bye kisses and apologetic looks. Her online gallery work could wait a little, she reasoned, and she didn't like messes—especially in the kitchen. So, she tied up her hair, decided to leave her current tank top on since it was already smudged with waffle batter, and got down to work. Even the floor needed mopping, thanks to a sticky spill of maple syrup.

At about the time she was done with all of the dishes and the cleaning—and she hadn't heard from either of the guys yet —the doorbell rang. She set her mop in the bucket and peeled off her gloves. The bell rang a second time as she approached the door. Ivy vaguely thought that she must look like a sweaty mess and smell like cleaning products, so she hoped it was no one important. Especially since the bell was ringing a third time as she reached for the knob. Whoever it was certainly seemed impatient. Holding her bright orange rubber gloves in one hand, she opened the door with the other and stared.

On the front porch stood an incredibly beautiful woman. She was tall, elegant, and thin, giving her the appearance of a high fashion model. Her hair was silvery blonde, her expertly made-up eyes were huge and cornflower blue, and there was something about her that was so ethereal it made Ivy wonder if the woman were about to blow away in a gust of wind. She was flanked by designer luggage, and Ivy was aware suddenly of a car pulling away from the house. She stared at the woman in shock.

"Oh," gasped the woman. "Uh...*hasta la vista*. Is *Señor* Bodhi Monaghan at *la casa* now?" she asked in the weirdest combination of inappropriate Spanish and English Ivy had ever heard. Ivy wondered if she spoke either language fluently.

She narrowed her eyes at the woman and answered, "No."

With a cross look on her face, the blonde asked loudly, "*Dónde está Señor* Bodhi? He... uh...lives-o here-o in this *casa*, right?"

"Pardon me miss, but who are you and what do you want with *Señor* Bodhi?" Ivy added the "*señor*" just to be sarcastic. Unfortunately, this had the wrong effect on the visitor.

"Oh, well, I can understand why he might not have confided in the housekeeper, but I'm his wife. Bring these bags in so I can get settled. *Por favor?* I really need to get off my feet and relax a moment. Thank God you speak English. You never know this close to the border."

Ivy felt her face burn and her knees knock. She didn't even care that the woman mistook her for a maid because all she heard was the word "wife." She thought she might faint dead away on the spot. Taking a step backward into the house, she stared dumbly at the blonde woman who seemed unaware of her surprise.

"I'm Blair Hendrix, of course," as if everyone should already know that, and Ivy's name was of no consequence. "Perhaps he told you I was on my way." She regarded Ivy's disheveled appearance and said, "It was nice of him to see that the house was cleaned before my arrival at least." Blair swept by Ivy in a miasma of cloying perfume that made Ivy's eyes itch. She recognized the smell at once; she had noticed it hanging on one of Bodhi's suits when they'd helped him move into the master closet. At the time, Ivy had chalked it up to a night out in a pub or something—surely nothing of importance.

"Boy, was I wrong," she muttered to herself. Ivy was sure she was going to puke any moment. She watched Blair's critical gaze take in everything around her.

Slowly, Ivy closed the door, leaving Blair's luggage on the porch. If Bodhi was married to this weirdo—albeit a beautiful one—and he wanted her there, *he* could bring in the bags himself. Ivy wanted no part of it. Mortified at the thought of his possible deceit, Ivy's eyes prickled with unshed tears. She would *not* let them fall. She'd already spent too many hours sobbing over that man, and just when things were rounding the corner toward looking good, Blair... his *fucking wife* shows up? It was impossible to comprehend the duplicity of the man. He'd probably been laughing at Cooper and her all along for their gullibility, when all he'd wanted was some dirty, kinky fun.

After eyeing the couch, apparently looking for signs of dust, Blair sat down and primly crossed her ankles. She looked questioningly at Ivy and demanded, "Well? Aren't you going to offer me some refreshment? A cold drink? Coffee?"

Giving Blair her best no-fucks-given look, Ivy answered, "Nope. I hadn't planned on it."

Spluttering a small ladylike gasp, Blair asked, "Aren't you worried you'll lose your job for insubordination? That means..."

"I fucking well understand the word, lady. And I'm not the least bit worried about losing my job since I run my own business."

Wrinkling her nose slightly, Blair cooed, "Oh! You have your own cleaning service? How enterprising of you."

"No, I don't own a cleaning service, though if I did, it's good, honest work and nothing to be demeaned. I live here. Permanently!" Ivy stomped out of the room and was dumping out the bucket of mop water when the back door opened, and Cooper burst in all full of smiles.

"Wait 'til you see Bodhi's new car. It's amazing!" Then he saw her stormy look and asked, "What's wrong?"

Stomping around for a second or two, she plonked the mop and bucket back into the broom closet and then turned, hands on hips, to tell him angrily, "Bodhi has a *guest*. She's in the living room—or she was when I left her. She's probably moved in by now. She says she's Bodhi's *wife*."

Cooper's face blanched. "Well shit," he whispered. "Are you sure?"

Ignoring his question, she asked, "Where is Bodhi?"

"He was right behind me, so unless he wanted to go show his new car off to someone else, he ought to be..." Just then, they heard the telltale sign of a car door closing, and they both glowered at the back door, waiting for it to open.

When it did open, Bodhi swept in with a goofy grin, exclaiming, "Man! It drives like a dream! Oh, Ivy, I'm glad you're right here. Come out and let me show it to you." When Ivy didn't move or stop glaring at him, he got a questioning look on his face. "What's wrong?" Then he looked at Cooper and saw a similar frown on his buddy's face, he asked, "What am I missing here? Is someone mad about losing their space in the garage or something? If so, we can add onto it and make it a three-car one. C'mon out and take a look, please?" Brightening, he added, "You're going to love this, Ivy!"

Finally, Ivy broke her silence and asked, "Wouldn't you rather show it to your *wife* first? She's waiting for you in the next room."

Bodhi's face fell. "Oh. Fuck. No."

Chapter Twelve

Bodhi felt himself break out into a nervous sweat, and before he could say anything else, his worst nightmare walked through the kitchen door with her arms outstretched toward him. She had a fake-as-sin smile plastered on her perfect face, and she stalked toward him like a lioness with her prey within grasp.

"Bodhi, darling," she cooed. "It's good to be here finally. I've missed you so much, sweetheart." She offered him her cheek to kiss, but Bodhi stepped backward until he was plastered against the back door. She approached closer, and he shrank from her as she leaned in for a kiss. He wrenched his head to the side so she couldn't collide with his lips. Ignoring his slight, she plowed on in a well-modulated and still pissed-off sounding voice, "You really ought to be hiring better help. This messy little woman has been rather insulting to me. And she claims she's a live-in? Really, darling, you need to be more discriminating."

Bodhi carefully took Blair's arms and moved her away from him and then snatched his hands back as if touching her was repugnant. "How did you find me?" he asked.

Ivy and Cooper looked at each other. This wasn't at all what they'd expected, and their eyes were full of questions.

Cooper had an immediate flash of hope that Blair would take Bodhi away from Ivy—but that meant he'd also be leaving *him*, and that was intolerable, so Cooper squelched that traitorous idea.

Ignoring Bodhi's obvious frustration with her, Blair asked smoothly, "What do you mean, darling? It was all in the papers you left for me."

"I didn't leave you any papers," Bodhi growled. "And I've blocked you from my phone."

Ivy sucked in her breath. She knew how painful it was to have Bodhi up and leave without much of an explanation, but to his *wife*? Unreal. He hadn't learned anything from past mistakes. Instead, he was pulling the same shit again on another woman. He must be the monster she thought he was after all. Her stomach began to ache with the memory of her own emotional pain caused by the heartless cad.

Bodhi looked as if the lights suddenly came on in his head and he asked, "You somehow managed to get into my apartment again, didn't you?" His voice grew in volume. "What did you do, Blair, blow the doorman?"

"Bodhi! Was that called for?" gasped Ivy. She may have taken an instant dislike to Blair, but still...

Bodhi swung around and glared at Ivy. "Yes. It was called for. You don't know her like I do." Then he jerked his face back to Blair and demanded, "What is this crap about being my *wife*? Who in their right mind would believe that?"

Ivy breathed a sigh of relief and grabbed Cooper's hand. Maybe things weren't as bad as they looked—just weird. Really, really weird.

Putting her chin in the air and straightening her shoulders, Blair declared, "I'm as good as your wife."

"Bullshit!" he bellowed.

"Well, if your friends hadn't gotten you drunk so you missed our wedding, it would have happened," she reasoned illogically. "And I'm pre..."

"More BS!" Bodhi interrupted her. "I told you time and time again that we were *not* getting married, and you carried on with that crazy charade. You sent out invitations and arranged an entire wedding even though at every possible opportunity I told you to stop."

"Nonsense, darling," she interrupted. "I understood you were just nervous and having normal second thoughts. It happens to all grooms, but I knew you would be there. If it hadn't been for those..."

With a look so cold it could freeze lava, Bodhi stopped her by saying through gritted teeth, "Blair!" He took a deep breath and continued, "I didn't go out and have a drunken bachelor party with anyone. I didn't show up to that sham of a wedding *on purpose.* Now get yourself out of my house and as far away from my friends as you can get. I don't ever want to see or hear from you again. Do I make myself clear?"

Blair simpered and batted her eyelashes at him before dropping the next bomb. "What about the baby? You'll want to be a good daddy for him, won't you?"

Bodhi scooted away from her like he'd been sucker-punched and collapsed in a kitchen chair. He leaned forward and put his head in his hands. He mumbled into them, "Please, Blair. Tell me this is just another one of your fucking lies and manipulation schemes. Tell me the truth for *once* in your horrible, twisted life."

Swooning, Blair grabbed for the kitchen counter and asked, "Where's the bathroom? I think I'm going to be sick. It must be the smell of the cleaning lady along with my regular morning sickness." She raised her free hand to cover her mouth.

Figuring someone had to take control while Bodhi and Ivy went catatonic, Cooper gently took her by the arm and led her to the hall bathroom. As soon as he closed the door on her, he heard retching. Not really knowing what to do, he waited until he heard the toilet flush and the tap going. He knocked lightly on the door. "Are you going to be okay?"

A moment later, Blair opened the door and peered out at him with watery eyes and a red face. She appeared unsteady on her feet when she asked breathily, "Is there somewhere I can lie down?"

"Uh... I guess you can have the guest... the... um... Bodhi's bedroom for a while. It's right here across the hall." He led her by the arm and watched while she did a dramatic swoon onto the bed, kicking off her high heels in an efficient move. She lay back and ordered, "I'll need some ice water and my bags, assuming a ruffian hasn't made off with them by now. The maid left them all outdoors." She let out a pained sigh and closed her eyes.

"Right. We have battling gangs of ruffians here in Del Mar. And they all camp out in Bodhi's front yard," he muttered sarcastically as he marched out the door. "It's a regular hooligan paradise here."

Nevertheless, Cooper dragged in Blair's luggage and dumped everything in a heap by the front door. Surveying the suitcases, he chose the smallest one that looked like something a woman might keep nearby and rolled it to the bedroom.

When Cooper returned with her suitcase, she asked in a wan voice, "Do you work for Bodhi too?"

Incredulous, he answered, "I'm Cooper—Bodhi's best friend."

"Oh. He never mentioned you," she replied sleepily with her eyes closed.

"Did he ever mention Ivy? She's pretty important to him."

"No," she whispered in a put-upon tone. She barely cracked one eye open and watched as Cooper turned toward the door.

Cooper thought that either Blair knew a lot less about Bodhi than she thought she did, or Bodhi was a real two-faced shit. Unfortunately, he wasn't completely sure which one was true. Cooper stomped out of the bedroom with no further comment.

Even retrieving her luggage was more interference into Bodhi's troubles than he wanted to pursue. Someone else could get the bitch some ice water. He was done with her.

* * *

Back in the kitchen, he found Bodhi red-faced and loudly defending himself to an equally scarlet Ivy.

"I have no idea why she thinks I fathered a kid with her!"

"Well, duh! Obviously, you've had sex with her."

Bodhi's eyes looked pained as he answered, "I might have, but if I did, I don't remember it."

"What?" asked Ivy and Cooper simultaneously. Then Ivy continued, "How can you say that? Did you sleep around with so many women, you can't remember them? That's disgusting, Bodhi! You weren't gone *that* long."

"No! Of course not. For the first ten months or so, I didn't do anything but work. I told you that. I barely had time to eat, sleep, and change my clothes. It was a ridiculous schedule, and I had no time for screwing around, believe me."

"And then?" asked Ivy. "At some point you must have made the acquaintance of the *lovely* Blair Hendrix who's... where is she, Cooper?"

"I left her sleeping in Bodhi's old room," he answered sheepishly. He thought of the nameless women whose beds he'd hopped into before his relationship with Ivy and decided to remain mute on that particular topic.

"Cooper, no! You left her alone in the house? She's completely nuts! You should have shoved her out the door. We have to get her out of here." Bodhi jumped up and began pacing around the kitchen as they stared at him. "But... oh god... what if this time she's telling the truth? What if she *is* having my baby? What am I going to do? I can't let her have my kid. I mean… sorry that's not what I mean… what I mean is, she can't *raise my kid!* She's a *horrible person.* I could never let that happen to a child."

Cooper took in his friend's obvious stress level and said, "From the looks of things, she's pretty out of it right now. My guess is she'll nap for a while. Let's all go outside where we won't wake her up, and you can tell us exactly how you know her and what happened, okay?"

* * *

So, sitting in his favorite outdoor chair, Bodhi launched into a tale of guile and deceit.

"I was working way too hard and too many hours, and something had to give. I was starting to worry that my judgment was compromised by lack of sleep. So, one afternoon, when a couple of people in the office suggested we knock off at a normal time and go to a pub, I agreed to go along. They were good people and needed a break by then as badly as I did, so at around seven that evening, we headed out."

Cooper snorted and asked, "You all called that an early quitting time?"

Bodhi nodded seriously. "Yeah. So anyway, the pub was crawling with people, and it was loud in there. We were all laughing, drinking our beers, and relaxing at last. I was telling them about what it was like learning to surf, and I noticed this woman a couple of tables over kept looking at me. She was definitely beautiful, but not my type." Bodhi looked at Ivy and said pointedly, "I prefer curvy little brunettes any day over skinny blondes. I always want to tell them to go eat something." He gave a rueful smile. "Anyway, you can guess—that was Blair. About three more beers and maybe an hour later, she came over to me and mentioned she was attracted to my American accent. She's from Arizona I think, but she'd been living in London with her aunt or some shit for a while. I'm still not sure why she stayed in London, because she didn't seem to be going to school and she didn't have a job. Maybe Arizona threw her out." He smiled ruefully at his dumb joke.

"I didn't want to be impolite, so we talked. It was flattering to have a beautiful woman hanging on every word I said, so when she asked if I'd like to get out of there, I said okay." He looked at them imploringly. "Please understand that I hadn't gotten laid in forever, so..." He paused for effect. "She couldn't take me back to her aunt's place, so we headed to my flat. It wasn't very far away."

Bodhi suddenly stood and said, "I want some water. Anyone else?" When they both nodded, he hurried into the kitchen and back out again with chilled bottles for everyone. He resumed his story.

"We got to my place, and, in retrospect, she probably seemed a little more impressed with it than was necessary. I mean, it's a nice place, but she looked like she came from money judging from the way she dressed. It shouldn't have been all that amazing to her." He sighed. "Anyway, she asked for the 'powder room'—who calls it that anyway? She took off to 'freshen up,' and I headed to my bedroom to get out of my suit. I was so sick of wearing a jacket and tie. You have to remember I hadn't eaten anything substantial other than a couple handfuls of bar nuts. The pub had pickled eggs too, but—you know... gross." He made a disgusted face. "Anyway, I'd been drinking for hours by then, so when I sat down on the bed to take off my shoes, the last thing I remember about the night was falling backward onto the bed. When my alarm went off the next morning at 5:30, I was in bed, naked as the day I was born, and Blair was in bed with me—also stark naked and sound asleep. So... it's possible that something happened between us. I have a vague recollection of some kissing, and that's it."

"So, what you're saying," Ivy clarified, "is that there was no evidence of a used condom? That would have been a good indication, but the absence of it could be really good or really bad."

"That's exactly what I'm saying. And, for the record, I got myself tested a while after this happened and, as I told you," he looked at Ivy, "I'm clean." Bodhi guzzled some water, letting them absorb the information for a moment. "Anyway, I got ready for work really quietly, thinking I'd avoid an uncomfortable encounter with her because, as both of you are well aware, I can be a complete chickenshit when it comes to stuff like that. Finally, I woke her up and asked her to get dressed. I let her know I'd called a car for her, and she had fifteen minutes to get her clothes on and head downstairs. I thanked her for the evening and explained that I had to get to the office right away. I figured I'd get something to eat on the way, and I sure as shit didn't want to have a breakfast date with her."

"How did she react to your brush-off?" Ivy asked. It sounded like a recipe for disaster to her.

"She was polite and friendly. Didn't seem at the time to be fazed by it, though she did try to kiss me goodbye. I wasn't having it, and that perturbed her. I mostly just wanted to get away from her." He shivered a little in the warm summer air. "She gave off the weirdest vibe that morning. In retrospect, it was probably insanity, but I just thought she might be hung-over and sleepy. Then too, there was the smell of her perfume. I hadn't noticed it the night before with all of the people crowded in the pub, but it was so strong and intense, and I had to stop myself from gagging like three times. Maybe she sprayed more on when she crawled into my bed... I don't know."

Ivy nodded understandingly. That perfume was *gross*. Then a thought struck her. "Why didn't she tell you she was pregnant before this? It seems pretty convenient, don't you think?" Before Bodhi could answer, she continued, "And when exactly did you meet her? Could they really determine the sex of the baby at this point? This sounds pretty fishy to me. Sorry, Bodhi. Go on with your story."

"I was pretty tired at work that day, so I cut out way earlier than usual. I actually left at five o'clock and headed home because I needed a solid meal and a good night's sleep so badly. But when I got home, it was to find that Blair not only hadn't left—she'd moved in."

Cooper and Ivy's jaws dropped. "Okay, so she really is nuts," Cooper muttered. "What did you do?"

"I called the building manager and gave him hell for allowing her back in, then I called the police who said they were not going to come and move her out and not to call them unless she actually broke in or became violent. They suggested that I needed to be more discriminating with my overnight guests in the future." He gave a sour look and continued, "Finally, I tried a different tactic and asked Blair politely to go out to have some dinner with me. She seemed happy about that but once we got to the restaurant, I ditched her and beat it back to my place. I dumped all of her shit out in the hall and told the super to come and get it and take it to the lobby. That seemed to work, and I thought I'd seen the last of her."

"I'm guessing you were incorrect," observed Cooper.

"You would be right."

Movement at the back window caught Ivy's attention and she tapped Bodhi's foot lightly with hers. He followed her gaze and muttered, "Aw, fuck."

Blair stood staring out at them. She composed her angry look into one of placid acceptance and wandered out toward them with a bottle of water in her hand. She gracefully lowered herself into the fourth chair and cracked open the top. Fixing Cooper with an annoyed stare, she asked, "Why didn't you bring me any water when I told you I was so parched?" Turning to Bodhi, she observed, "You really ought to keep company with a better sort of people, darling. These two have been unspeakably rude."

Ignoring her insult, Cooper turned to Ivy and asked, "How would you like to join me over at my parents' place? They've been trying to get us over there forever. I think Bodhi and Blair need some time to sort things out, and this is a prime opportunity."

He raised his eyebrows at Ivy who popped up out of her chair and answered, "Great idea. I'll just go run and change quickly." She gave Bodhi a look that said she was mildly sorry and left the patio.

Bodhi immediately looked panicked. *Left alone with Blair? Now what?* Then he gave Blair a long, skeptical look. "How come you don't look pregnant, Blair?"

Her entire countenance went rigid, but she answered in a flowery soft voice, "Silly man. It takes time to show. Lots of women don't even have a pooch until around four months, so of course I'm not showing yet." She gave him a saccharine smile.

After no one spoke to Blair for a few minutes, she started breathing heavily and clutched her tummy with a dramatic sigh. Putting her other hand over her mouth, she groaned through her fingers, "Pardon me, darling. I'm going to be sick again." She rose and sauntered back into the house while the two men watched her retreat in silence.

Chapter Thirteen

Ivy took a quick, fortifying shower and rushed out of the en suite master bathroom, planning to get dressed and out of the house in a hurry. Nearly jumping out of her skin, she shrieked, "What the hell are you doing in here?"

Blair sat on the foot of the bed staring at Ivy's naked body with a scornful, assessing expression. "Really, dear. I think you've been eating too many tacos lately."

"Get the fuck out of my bedroom!" Ivy scooted into the closet and grabbed for something to put on. She yanked on underwear and then a skirt and top in record time. Exiting the closet, she realized Blair hadn't moved a muscle.

"I thought I might clear the air with you a bit first," Blair announced in a sickly, sweet tone. "I'm sure you must realize how confused Bodhi is."

Screwing up her face, Ivy asked, "What are you talking about? He sounded pretty sure of himself to me."

Blair got a dreamy look on her face and asked, "Did he tell you about the lovely candlelit dinner we had when he proposed?"

"Nope. He said he ditched you in a restaurant and dumped your stuff in the hall."

Shaking her head in apparent amusement, Blair said with a chuckle, "Oh that man. He was probably embarrassed that I didn't accept his proposal right away. He's just saving face. In fact, he helped me move in—he was so desperate to have me with him full-time."

"Huh?"

"Oh yes. And I made him ask three times before I accepted his proposal. It was so fast, you know. And then he wanted the ceremony to happen immediately. He's such a hopeless romantic, that one."

"Bodhi? Hopeless romantic?" It was so un-Bodhi-like that Ivy almost laughed. She stared at Blair. *How can Blair look so ethereally beautiful and unruffled?* Ivy had no idea. She did wonder aloud, however, "If Bodhi was so anxious to marry you, why did he quit his job and beat it back here?"

Blair's laughter sounded like tinkling bells—and very practiced. "He said he quit? That's rich. He was fired, for your information, because he was taking too much time off of work to spend it at home, and *in bed* with me. He said he had to come back here where he had a place to live because he lost his flat, and that I was supposed to follow him as soon as I could tie up loose ends. He's obviously terribly embarrassed about his situation."

"If Bodhi's such a loser, why do you want to marry him so badly?" Ivy asked. She privately wondered about Bodhi's apartment. He hadn't said anything about giving it up. In fact, he'd alluded to needing to get out of the lease.

"Marry him? Who said I wanted to do that after finding out he'd lost his job? I had to say I was his wife so you would let me in the door. Like I said, I was exhausted." She touched her stomach and looked at Ivy with a pitiful expression. "Being pregnant is hard, you know."

"I don't buy it," Ivy said. "You seemed pretty committed to the wedding you mentioned."

Blair sighed dramatically. "Look, I'm just giving Bodhi the opportunity to man up and take care of his child, that's all. If you want the truth, he's going to have to work at it if he wants a relationship with me." Blair looked across the room and caught her reflection in the mirror. She ran a graceful hand through her hair as if to smooth it—even though it already looked perfect.

Now Ivy was completely confused. Bodhi's claim about quitting never sounded quite right, but he was obviously not interested in having Blair around. Then there was the baby issue. Ivy felt a headache coming on and couldn't wait to get to Cooper's parents' house. They were always so warm and welcoming. She was beginning to wonder if Bodhi was just using them for sex, and it made her feel sick. He told them both he loved them. *Was that a lie? Thank goodness I didn't say it back. That would be just one more humiliation with that man.*

Whatever the truth was, Ivy knew their triad fun was likely to end immediately or at the very least take a backseat to this drama. A strange sadness came over her at the thought; she didn't realize quite how much their relationship had come to mean to her. Ivy shook herself off and ducked back into the closet for some sandals. As she slipped them on, she announced, "Cooper and I will be back later."

"Wait," Blair commanded. Ivy looked at her questioningly. "Aren't you going to put on fresh makeup? Your... Mediterranean complexion could use a bit of brightening up and smoothing out, you know." She flapped her hand gracefully toward her own face—apparently to demonstrate how one should look at all times—and then added, "I guess the problem lies with your genes."

Ivy bristled and seethed, "You have no idea what my genes are, lady. And if I want to wear makeup or not, it's my decision. Cooper... *and* Bodhi both like me just fine the way I am, so quit being so condescending and fuck the hell off." She thundered out of the room and down the hall where she almost crashed into Cooper. She grabbed his arm and said, "Let's get out of here."

Chapter Fourteen

Bodhi, who was unaware of the drama in the house, sat in the patio with his head in his hands. He heard the sound of high-heeled footsteps approaching and wanted to crawl into a hole. A chilly hand touched his shoulder and he quickly shrugged it off.

"I have something wonderful to show you, darling."

He couldn't imagine anything remotely wonderful she might have, but he looked up with resignation written all over his face.

Blair scooted one of the patio chairs next to his and sat, holding out a piece of paper to him. "Look at this, darling. Isn't it just perfect? I had this done right before I left London."

Blinking, Bodhi took the sheet of paper and sucked in a breath. "Ohmygod," he whispered. In his hands he held a grainy black and white image of an ultrasound. His hand shook as he stared at it, and then finally he said, "This is beautiful. May I keep it?"

With the sweetest look on her face, Blair agreed, "Of course, darling. I have another copy. I've decided to call him Bodhi Junior."

He narrowed his eyes at her and asked, "How do you know it's a boy?"

"Oh, just intuition. I know the doctor said it was too early to tell, but... I have a feeling."

Bodhi reluctantly felt his walls crumbling and his defenses collapsing. If he...no *they* were going to have a baby, he needed to step up. Instantly he went into crisis mode. "Blair, what kind of health insurance do you have? Do I need to take care of that for you?"

Looking chagrined, Blair demurred. "Yes, darling. That would be most welcome. Since I'm back in the States for good, I'll need proper healthcare for us. Is it too expensive for you, though? Maybe I can go to a free clinic or something."

"It's fine, Blair. I'll make sure you and the baby get the best healthcare possible. You can count on me for that." He looked at her hopeful face and added, "I still don't want to be in a relationship with you, though. Don't get any ideas about us because of the baby."

She stroked his bicep and purred, "We'll see. You might come around and change your mind." He slowly scooted away from her touch as she continued, "You can't have become involved with anyone in the short time you've been back without me, so I don't really see any impediment to our being together the way we want."

"I know what I want, Blair, and I'm not trying to be mean when I say it isn't you. I'll want to have a paternity test done and then if I am the dad, I'd like to establish full custody."

Blair reared back as if he'd slapped her across the face. "No way!" she cried. "You would take a baby from his mother?"

Looking at her mulishly, he stated, "We can set up visitation rights. But you know as well as I that I'd make the better parent."

Blair let all of her frustration evaporate and answered meekly, "I suppose you're right. You're so much smarter than I am."

Bodhi couldn't believe her sudden capitulation or her mood swings, but he'd heard Cooper's younger sister talk about pregnancy hormones messing with your thinking, and he considered Blair's natural state of imbalance. Squinting at her thoughtfully he asked, "Do you want me to find you a doctor?"

Quickly, she answered, "Oh, no thank you. My specialist, um...OB-GYN, in London has already referred me to someone, and I have an appointment in a couple of weeks."

That sounded odd to Bodhi, but what did he know about having babies? "I'll go with you to the appointment," he said in a no-nonsense voice.

"Don't be silly. That won't be necessary. You'd be bored."

"On the contrary, Blair. I think hearing *my* baby's heartbeat and talking to the doctor about what to expect will be extremely interesting." He saw a flash of some emotion flit across her features, but he couldn't discern its meaning. It was gone just as quickly as it came. "So, it's settled then. Let me know the time of the appointment and I'll make sure to take you."

* * *

When Cooper and Ivy returned that night, it was late. They hadn't known what to expect, but they were mildly surprised to find the house quiet, and Bodhi sacked out on the couch sound asleep under a spare blanket.

"I guess Blair's still here," Ivy observed. "Too bad."

They approached him quietly, and Cooper reached out to tap Bodhi's shoulder. "Hey, man," he whispered, "want to join us tonight? You don't need to sleep out here."

Groggily, Bodhi sat up and yawned. Sighing, he answered, "Look, I'd like to—you both know that. But I told Blair I want custody of the kid, so until I can get her out of the house and into her own place, I want to look like the model dad, you know? All she knows is that the room she's in now was my room, and I don't want to sleep in it with her."

Pouting, Ivy stuck out her lower lip and said, "We'll miss you." She kissed Bodhi soundly on the lips and grabbed Cooper's hand.

Cooper resisted for a second and then also leaned over and kissed Bodhi and said, "If you change your mind, you know where to find us."

Chapter Fifteen

To say that things were tense for the next several days is like pointing out that the Pacific Ocean is wet and salty.

Ivy attempted to ignore Blair's constant snipes about her appearance. She knew Blair's intent was to make her feel insecure, but despite herself, it was working. Blair never did it in front of the guys, and Ivy never told them about it. Ivy knew that Bodhi had a lot on his mind, and he didn't need to run interference for something Ivy should be able to handle. She told herself to deal with Blair on her own.

Cooper pretended to be polite to Blair's face, but he couldn't stop himself from muttering insults under his breath that she couldn't hear. It irked him that she never lifted a finger to help out around the house, even though she seemed to think it was her right to move in and stay there. She seemed to spend an inordinate amount of time lying down. He knew pregnancy could wear a woman out, but this was ridiculous.

Bodhi tried to act as if having Blair around was not driving him batshit crazy. He scoured every source he could find for possible alternate housing, but summertime at the beach with the Del Mar racing season quickly approaching made it almost impossible to find another place.

A few times, after consulting his laptop, Bodhi would whoop for joy and grab Blair to go see something that was available, only to return an hour later in a foul mood. "I can't imagine why you didn't like that one," he exclaimed after their most recent trip.

"Did you see the mold in the bathroom? Bodhi, really! How can you think I could live there like that?"

"It was a dark spot on the shower door, Blair. It may not have even been mold!"

"I can't take any chances with an unhealthy environment. You should understand that, darling."

"Living near the beach makes things mold sometimes, you know. There are cleaning products for it."

Blair shuddered visibly and announced, "I need to go lie down."

* * *

And that was how things went—over and over. He was even willing to put her up in a hotel at an exorbitant price, but they were all booked solid.

Outside of prying her out of his house with a crowbar, Bodhi was running out of ideas. He did, however, get her set up with a fantastic health insurance plan that was going to cost him an arm and a leg. He looked at it as an investment in his baby's good health.

After she'd been at the house for a couple of weeks, driving them all insane, she announced to Bodhi, "Tomorrow is my appointment. And really—you don't need to come. It won't be much more than me getting to know the doctor."

"Why don't you want me to accompany you?" he asked with narrowed eyes.

"Of course I want you to go with me, but I'm just afraid you'll be bored," she answered smoothly as she reached out to stroke his arm. Bodhi pulled out of her reach.

Glaring at her, he explained once again, "I won't be bored. I'm looking forward to it." And he was. He'd practically stared a hole in the ultrasound image she'd given him. It looked rather like a tiny alien or Mr. Peanut in there, but the sight of his future offspring warmed his heart. Bodhi had fantasies about teaching his son to pitch a baseball, ride a bike, and—best of all—surf. He thought about what it would be like to have a mini-Bodhi running around the house and decided they also were going to need a sweet golden retriever for the kid to love and to learn responsibility with. He'd teach the boy to feed his pup and they'd all go for walks together or runs on the beach.

Bodhi had it all figured out. Unfortunately, he was an only child with rather independent parents who'd moved to Hawaii when they discovered that Bodhi would be living in England. He wouldn't have much in the way of family moral support from anyone except—hopefully—Ivy and Cooper. He didn't have the slightest idea what it would be like to raise a kid, but the rose-colored-glasses ideal sounded pretty cool to him. So, during the lonely nights when he tried to be comfortable enough to sleep on the couch, he dreamed of his future life with his child.

At breakfast one morning, Bodhi announced to Cooper, "I'm getting rid of the gym equipment in the third bedroom."

"Finally sick of the couch?" Cooper asked with a knowing smirk.

Bodhi blinked as if the thought hadn't occurred to him and answered, "No. I'm turning the room into a nursery. It'll be great. I was looking online, and they have a lot of these cool things for babies now like dinosaur mobiles and that kind of shit. You can even decorate the ceiling with glow-in-the-dark constellations."

"Always practical, aren't you?" Cooper said with a laugh. "Did it ever occur to you that it would be more important to have a crib, a changing table, and a diaper pail? Don't let me burst your bubble, though." Cooper had nieces and nephews, so he was familiar with the drill.

"Oh yeah, of course. I just want the kid to have fun, you know?"

Pouring a cup of coffee, Cooper asked, "Bodhi, think about it. What if this isn't even your kid? Aren't you getting a little ahead of yourself?"

"Yeah, I guess," he answered, but he didn't look happy as he turned to stare out the window.

A few minutes later, just as Cooper was heading out for work, Blair showed up in the kitchen. Though this was a lot earlier than her normal wake-up time, she was dressed impeccably, and her makeup was flawless. "Good morning, darling. Are you excited about our appointment later?" she asked Bodhi. "It's in an hour."

"I am for sure," he smiled and looked genuinely happier than he had in a while.

"You seem to be out of coffee," Blair observed looking into his mug. "Want another? I'm just going to pour one for myself."

Bodhi thought she must be in a good mood to actually lift a finger for someone else, but he scooted his mug closer to her and said, "Sure. Thanks." He stood and loaded his breakfast dishes into the dishwasher and was cleaning out the frying pan from the eggs he'd fixed when Blair set down the coffee for him. She turned to make some toast for herself.

Bodhi took a healthy gulp of the coffee that appeared to be liberally laced with cream. He wasn't at all worried that it would be too hot with all of that cold liquid in it. Choking down the swallow, however, he spluttered, "What did you do, Blair? Empty the sugar bowl in this? Or is this some of that awful artificial sweetener? Gross." He stood and threw the remaining coffee into the sink. "Thanks for trying, but I just take it with cream and no sugar. I thought you knew."

"Oh, sorry, darling. I guess I mixed up the two cups." She laughed disparagingly at herself. "Pregnancy brain, you know? Ever since I started expecting our baby, I've craved mine extra sweet. Here, take this one instead. I'll make another pot since that was all there was of the coffee."

"No thanks. I've sort of lost my taste for it after that. I think I'll just go brush my teeth and get ready to leave. He rinsed the mug and loaded it into the dishwasher, but when he leaned over to place the cup, he felt strange—nauseous and dizzy all of a sudden. And he was sweating profusely. *I'll need to put on a different shirt*, he thought.

He took off down the hall and almost ran into Ivy. She looked stunning in a bright blue sundress with her hair piled on top of her head and a few tendrils accenting her lovely face. Her cleavage was just apparent enough to tease, but still sedate enough for a work day. He wanted to start kissing her and never quit. But when he opened his mouth to compliment her, he suddenly knew he had to make it to the bathroom— and *fast*.

"Bodhi? What's wrong? You look terrible," Ivy gasped.

He didn't even have the time to close the door as he lunged toward the commode. Immediately his breakfast reappeared with a vengeance.

After a lot of retching, Bodhi looked at a very stricken Ivy who handed him a cold, wet washcloth. "Are you going to be okay?" she asked. "Should I get my assistant to cover for me today so I can stay with you?"

Bodhi took the cloth gratefully and wiped his face off with it. In a raspy voice he assured her, "I'm sure it's just a quick stomach bug, Ivy. I was perfectly fine until this happened." He closed his eyes for a second and seemed to sway on his feet a little. "I'll be all right. I just need to go lie down."

"Well, if you're sure. But don't go lie down on that darn sofa. Take our bed in the big bedroom, okay?" She felt his forehead and noted that he was clammy rather than hot. "I'll bring you some ginger ale and some crackers for later. Go lie down now." She shooed him out of the bathroom and went to find him some supplies.

"Ivy?" Bodhi called out weakly. "Can you ask Blair to come and talk to me for a minute, please? She's in the kitchen."

A couple of minutes after Bodhi stripped down to a clean t-shirt and boxers and slipped into the comfortable bed, Blair crept into the room. She held a bottle of ginger ale and a box of crackers. Bodhi cracked open one eye and looked at her in the dim light.

She set the stuff down on the bedside table and said officiously, "I'm sorry you're under the weather, but I thought you might like these when you start feeling better."

Bodhi gave a sad chuckle and asked, "Are you sure Ivy didn't send you in here with those? That sounds an awful lot like what she said to me before she left."

"Oh, well, um... everyone knows that you need these for an upset stomach."

"Never mind, Blair. It doesn't matter. I don't think I can make it to your appointment today under the circumstances." He eyed her for any emotion and detected a small sense of relief as he thought, *Is she really so embarrassed about seeing her doctor with me along? It makes no sense. I'd think most women would want a partner along for moral support, even if they weren't together.* Aloud, he asked, "Would you rather take a ride share or my car?"

"Oh! You'd be okay if I borrowed your car?"

"Not normally, no. But I understand you need to get there pretty soon, and there may not be enough time to call a car now. I'm sorry I can't drive you." Bodhi inwardly shuddered with the thought of her driving his new toy. Then his shudders turned real, and he jumped up and ran to the bathroom for another bout of being sick. When he could finally gather himself together enough to make it back to bed, he found Blair sitting and waiting for him.

"Can I do anything else for you before I leave?" she asked sweetly.

Bodhi wondered why she looked so serene and satisfied, but he chalked it up to her insanity. He retrieved his car key from his discarded pants and handed it to her, swaying slightly. "Do you know how to get driving directions?"

"Of course, silly." She happily snatched the key and scooted out of the room.

He called out weakly to her, "Be careful." Wondering if she'd even heard him, Bodhi flopped back into bed and hoped he'd start feeling better soon. Within minutes, he was asleep.

Several hours went by, and when Bodhi awoke, he felt almost normal. He realized he was hungry and reached for the crackers. In doing so, he saw on the clock that it was well past noon, so certainly Blair would be back by now with some news. He wolfed down a handful of crackers and chugged the lukewarm ginger ale. It had a calming effect on his stomach, and he was happy to feel so improved after such a short time. *What a weird bug*, he thought. *But there always seems to be something new going around.* Finally, he got up, pulled on a pair of shorts, and wandered down the hall barefoot in search of Blair.

She wasn't in her room, so he tried the rest of the house. Nope. She was nowhere to be found. He checked and discovered his car was also still gone. Stymied, he fetched his phone and looked up the contact he'd blocked for her. He unblocked and then called it, and it went to voicemail immediately.

When another hour went by and she still hadn't returned, Bodhi started to pace the house. *Where the hell can she be? No doctor's appointment takes this many hours.* Trying to decide what to do, he went outside and sat in the sunny patio where he always felt the best. He even considered grabbing his board and hiking down to the beach, but he was afraid he was still too weak and would disgrace himself after being so sick all morning.

...And then his phone rang. Snatching it up, he didn't even look at the caller ID when he asked frantically, "Blair?"

He heard a soft chuckle and then a familiar voice say, "No, you big goofball. It's Ivy. How are you feeling? Any better?"

"Oh, Ivy. Yeah, I'm feeling lots better. I don't know what that was, but I barfed it out and slept it off. Maybe it was some kind of food poisoning."

"Hmm. Didn't we all eat the same stuff last night though? Anyway, doesn't matter. I'm just happy and relieved to know you're better. I called because I have some potentially great news for you."

Bodhi brightened quickly and asked, "What's that?"

"My friend Casey came into the gallery today. I've been asking around for you to everyone I've come into contact with lately, and Casey says he knows of someone out in Rancho Santa Fe who has a guest house on their property that they want to rent out. It's only a couple of years old, fully furnished, and he says he's seen it and it's really nice. If Casey says it's nice, it's probably gorgeous. Best of all, it's ready now, so Blair could move right in." She lowered her voice, even though she was currently alone in the gallery and added, "She can get the fuck out of your hair, and we can get back to..." she cleared her throat, "normal. Isn't that great?"

There was no response.

"Bodhi?"

Bodhi had heard everything Ivy said, but before he could reply, Blair came through the back door looking even paler than usual. It looked like she had been crying. He had a terrible feeling about this. The phone clattered onto the table as he went to Blair and escorted her gently to a chair.

Ivy could hear Bodhi asking, "Are you all right? Can I get you anything? Is the baby okay? What's going on, Blair? You're scaring me."

Then his voice came back on the line, and he said clearly to Ivy, "I need to call you back. Thanks. Bye." And the line went dead.

Bodhi looked frantically at Blair who seemed to have shrunken in on herself. Her eyes looked flat, and she was paler than he'd ever seen her. "What's the matter?" he asked her in as gentle a voice as he could muster.

Eventually Blair seemed to rally a little and looked at him. "I'm sorry, darling. I've failed you."

"What are you talking about?" Bodhi felt his blood run cold. "Did you miscarry? Is there something wrong with the baby?"

"No, I did not miscarry. I've been driving around and thinking how I'd break the news to you, and I didn't get any ideas, so I'll just say it."

"What?" he demanded.

"It's not... not a *boy*."

Bodhi jerked back. "*That's* what you're crying about? You think I care?"

"Well, all men want a son. I thought how special it would be if I gave you that. I thought it would make you..." Her voice dropped to a barely audible whisper, "Love me."

"Blair, I barely know you. We've never had any kind of a relationship, and I am not even particularly attracted to you. I'm sorry if that's harsh, but it's the truth. I'll take care of you and the baby, but I'll never love you the way you want me to. I can't. I'm..."

She narrowed her eyes at him and hissed out venomously, "It's because of that fat little... ethnic woman, isn't it?"

"What fat ethnic woman are you talking about?" He was completely befuddled and once again shocked by her violent mood change.

"I see you ogling her when you think I'm not paying attention." She sniffed. "She's an engaged woman, darling. Not exactly someone to pine after."

"You're talking about Ivy?" he spluttered. "First of all, she's not fat, she's perfect. Second of all, what ethnic group do you think she belongs to that deserves your derision?" He raised his hand and amended his question. "No, don't answer that because there *isn't* one! And furthermore, my feelings for her are none of your business, so shut the fuck up about her."

Blair seemed to swoon again and announced, "I need to go lie down."

Bodhi shook his head and clenched and unclenched his hands a few times. He was a mess. This woman had the power to make him nuts just by looking at him sometimes, but the vitriol and crazy shit that poured out of her mouth made his blood boil. He finally looked at her defeated face and tried to soften his emotions.

"Look, Blair, I'm okay that it's not a boy. I'd never hold that against you, for Chrissake. That's just ridiculous. And I just got some good news." He smiled at her encouragingly. "Ivy called and she knows of a great guest house in Rancho Santa Fe we could rent for you. It's beautiful out there—nice and quiet and away from the damp beach air that might make things mold. It sounds perfect. I'll have to call her back and get more details, but how about if we go see it tomorrow? It'll give you a chance to relax for the rest of today. You look like you could use it."

Her head snapped up and she glared at him. "Are you saying I look awful?"

"No, of course not. You're as beautiful as always," he said dismissively. "Have you had anything to eat? I can make you some soup and a sandwich and then you can take a nap. Sound good?"

"Oh, thank you, darling. Maybe just a little soup? I'll be in my room." With that, she disappeared back into the house, looking a bit unsteady on her feet.

Bodhi thought it a bit odd that she hadn't asked how he was feeling after his dramatic illness earlier that morning, but maybe it was obvious to her. He went in to make some food. As he prepared the late lunch for them, visions of a little blonde girl in a tutu skipping off to ballet class filled his head. He knew there was still the possibility of surfing with a daughter, and that sounded like fun, but there might also be tea parties and teddy bears. The dinosaur mobile was instantly replaced in his head with unicorns and sparkles. He smiled to himself as he stirred the pot. This would be great, and he knew he could be a terrific daddy. A daughter! The golden retriever still sounded good too. Every little girl needed a pet to cuddle and love.

He brought a tray into Blair's room a few minutes later and found her sleeping. Softly, he called out to her, "Blair? I brought you the soup. It's warm, so you'll want to eat it before it cools. I'll just leave it here on the bedside table, and I'll come to get your dishes in a little while."

She sat up groggily and looked at the tray with as much interest as she'd have had if it held a bowl of sand. "Thanks," she mumbled.

Bodhi had just exited the door when a thought struck him. "Hey, Blair, did you get another ultrasound photo today?" He turned back toward her with a hopeful expression and realized she had lain back down. She'd turned away from the food.

"No ultrasound today," she muttered weakly. "Going back to sleep now."

Bodhi sighed with disappointment and went to get a bit of work done. It wasn't until many hours later that it dawned on him to wonder just how Blair had found out she wasn't having a boy.

* * *

When Cooper and Ivy arrived home that evening, Bodhi was encouraged to see that Blair had not only roused herself from bed for once, she managed to help set the table and was moderately cordial to everyone throughout the dinner they all had together. Bodhi felt his senses on high alert the entire time, however, hoping and praying that she wouldn't go off like a Roman candle at something ridiculous. He also noticed that she didn't eat much of the delicious pasta dish that Ivy had put together for them. She ate a few nibbles of salad and seemed to push the pasta around her plate while rolling her eyes at Ivy each time the woman had a bite of food. *Oh well*, he thought. *At least she's not saying anything derogatory for once.*

Ivy had a lot to say about the guest house in Rancho Santa Fe, and she delivered the information with enthusiasm. "The residents of the estate only live there half of the time, and they built the guest house for the wife's widowed mother to move into. The mother decided to move to Argentina instead because she's reconnected with an old friend who convinced her that was the place for both of them to be." Ivy shrugged and laughed softly. "Take a look at these photos of the cottage my friend Casey sent me." Smiling, she passed her phone around so everyone could admire the place.

Blair was polite, though not overly enthusiastic. It grated on Bodhi that Blair never once even thanked Ivy for the effort she'd gone to on her behalf. Sighing inwardly, he realized he was expecting too much from a woman who thought about no one but herself. He wondered, not for the first time, if he was doing the right thing by taking care of someone he didn't like and barely knew, but if it was true that the baby she carried was his, he felt he had no choice. Each time he'd tried to press her for information about her family, she clammed up or changed the subject. Apparently, there would be no assistance from them.

He wished he could at least remember having sex with Blair. It seemed so strange to have such a clouded memory of that night. He guessed exhaustion could do that to a person. There was certainly no way to prove he hadn't fucked her. Eventually the paternity test would let him know. But in all honesty, the thought of being a dad was so appealing he wasn't sure he'd even go through with having the test done. Someone had to be a dad to the kid. *At least I have a while to decide and get used to the idea*, he reasoned with himself.

As soon as the dinner was over, Blair left without a word and headed to her room. Bodhi assumed she was exhausted again. He was just as happy when he, Cooper, and Ivy picked out a movie to watch together. He knew it wouldn't lead to sexy times for them, but the closeness of their company warmed his heart. *Soon*, he thought, *we can be together again without worrying about Blair in the next room.*

Chapter Sixteen

Early the next morning before anyone in the house had woken up, Bodhi was roused from sleep by the doorbell. He dragged himself off the couch, wrapped his blanket around his semi-dressed body, and was startled by the sight of two uniformed police officers at the door.

"Can I help you?" he asked in a froggy, early-morning voice as he squinted at them.

"Sorry to bother you so early, sir," one officer said. "Are you Bodhi Monaghan?"

"I am. What's going on?"

"May we come in, sir? We have some rather disturbing news for you," the other policeman said.

"Um... sure. Let me just get rid of this, and um..." he picked up his pillow and his pants and shirt from where he'd draped them over the arm of the couch. "Please have a seat, and I'll be right back." Bodhi dashed into the hall bathroom and re-appeared a few minutes later with his clothes on this time. *No one wants to talk to the police in their underwear*, he reasoned.

Just then, Cooper wandered down the hall looking mussed from sleep and curious about the doorbell. He'd gotten dressed too, Bodhi noted—pants *and* a shirt for once.

"What's going on?" Cooper asked. "I heard the doorbell and voices..." He had a distinct what-the-fuck look on his sleepy face.

"No idea. Let's find out," Bodhi said grimly.

After introductions, Officer Prue announced to Bodhi, "A car that is registered to you was towed off of the Coronado Bridge earlier this morning. It's in this impound lot where you can retrieve it." He produced a card with an address and phone number on it and eyed Bodhi carefully as Bodhi took it with an incredulous expression. All of the color in Bodhi's face seemed to have drained away as he waited for more information.

Officer Everts continued with the story in a kind but businesslike voice. "Witnesses saw the car pull off to the side and they reported that a woman stepped out. They described her as blonde and very thin, tall—maybe five-foot-nine or thereabouts. Given the high rate of suicides on that bridge, locals are quite vigilant about any suspicious behavior. Three different witnesses said they saw a man also pull up behind her and call out to her as she approached the wall. The woman, however, ignored his calls and climbed over the edge without looking back once and jumped to her death. I'm very sorry to have to tell you this. Do you know who she might be, and how she had your car? There was no ID on her body or in the car."

A noise like a dying elephant roared out of Bodhi's throat as he dashed to his old bedroom and wrenched the door open. The room was empty, which was no surprise.

Cooper ran after Bodhi and grabbed for him as Bodhi slumped to the floor. He put his arms around his buddy and let Bodhi cry into his chest.

"She killed my baby!" Bodhi hollered in agony. "And it was my fault, Cooper! I told her I didn't want her and wasn't attracted to her. Ohmygod, I killed them both!" He howled and gasped for breath as misery tore through his body.

Ivy also came out at that point and saw the devastation that used to be Bodhi sobbing in Cooper's arms. She'd heard what Bodhi said and looked at Cooper with grief-filled eyes for an explanation. He jerked his head toward the officers in the living room.

Gradually, Bodhi stopped wailing and choking and calmed down enough to answer the officers' many questions. Ivy and Cooper moved Bodhi to the couch where they could both hold onto him, and the story of how Blair came to live at the house unfolded for the officers' benefit in fits and bursts.

One question had them all shrugging their shoulders. Officer Prue asked, "I take it the two of you were not sharing a bed. But how did you miss that Ms. Hendrix passed through here at some point during the night? She had to have gotten your car key at the very least. Are you an extremely sound sleeper?"

Shaking his head, Bodhi answered, "I let her borrow the car yesterday, and I forgot to get the key back from her with all of her usual drama going on. Either I slept through her walking by me, or she snuck out at some point while I was in the bathroom. That's the only explanation I can give—oh, unless she climbed out the window. But that doesn't seem like her style."

"You never know," intoned Officer Everts. "She had to climb over the bird spikes on the wall to jump off the bridge. She must have been pretty determined."

"Bird spikes?" asked Ivy.

Everts answered, "A few years ago a committee formed to try to decrease the number of suicides on that bridge. They thought installing rows of long, sharp spikes on top of the bridge wall would deter the would-be jumpers. Unfortunately, all it did was make them jump sooner rather than sit on the railing a while and think about it. It didn't work at all to deter them, and the numbers have remained constant. It's sad. All it accomplished was keeping birds away." He looked solemnly at Bodhi and asked, "May we take a look at her belongings? It's possible she left a note somewhere."

Sure enough, the bedroom window was open, and the screen lay on the ground just outside. She hadn't been taking any chances that she'd be thwarted.

Even with the open window, Officer Prue asked with a screwed-up face, "What's that smell in here?"

In unison, Bodhi, Cooper, and Ivy intoned disgustedly, "Blair's perfume."

They also noted that a piece of paper sat beside the bed, and on it were the handwritten words:

It's better this way, darling.

No one knew what that meant other than she'd been determined to take her life for her own twisted reasons. Seeing it brought a new bout of crying and swearing by poor Bodhi. He'd just about reached his limit thinking about the poor innocent baby who'd been the victim of Blair's insane reasoning. *Just because she wasn't a boy?* he wondered.

"I know one thing for sure," he rasped out. "I never want to be called 'darling' by anyone for the rest of my life." He shuddered.

* * *

The officers sifted through Blair's belongings and didn't come up with much of interest—except for one thing. They couldn't find anything that gave them a clue to her background, but they found a small, partially full bottle of ipecac syrup hidden in the toe of a shoe.

Prue asked, "Why would a pregnant woman want to induce vomiting? This stuff is horrible. And why would she try to hide it?"

Bodhi plunked down on the bed and put his head in his hands. Everything was giving him a headache, and this was just one more reason to feel like his life was a crazy shitstorm. He looked up with red-rimmed eyes and answered shakily, "Yesterday Blair had an appointment with her OB-GYN, and I wanted to go with her to find out more about the baby and maybe hear the heartbeat." He cleared his throat and took a fortifying breath as he thought to himself about the innocent baby girl that was no longer. With a break in his voice he continued, "She wasn't too crazy about the idea, and I have absolutely no idea why. But... I was feeling fine yesterday until she handed me a horrible tasting cup of coffee. After one swallow, I threw the rest out, and shortly after that I got sick as a dog." He sighed. "I think that's your answer. She wanted me to stay home for some reason." He scoffed, "She could have just put her foot down and said no. She didn't have to try to poison me!" When another bout of grief struck him, he covered his face with his hands and shook silently.

Ivy looked thoughtful and wondered aloud, "That might have been what was in the small package she received the other day. I asked her what it was, and she told me it was 'pre-natal vitamins.' I never saw her take anything with her meals, though, so it may have been the ipecac. It's too bad the trash went out two days ago, or we'd be able to look at the pack-aging. It never occurred to me that she'd try to hurt Bodhi—she claimed to be deeply in love with him." She paused and then added, "Though I will say, it seemed more like desperate fixation than love."

After their search of the room was completed, Officer Everts asked, "Would you characterize the deceased as a depressed person? It's hard to think what would drive a young, pregnant woman to take her own life."

"More like bat-shit crazy and delusional than depressed," Bodhi answered ruefully. "I know Blair had to have mental problems, and it was my intent to establish custody and raise the child on my own. The thought of her caring for a baby gave me chills. Maybe she was more maternal than I gave her credit for, but... I don't know. She just never appeared to understand reality versus her own weird take on things. Obviously, she had no problem ending the baby's life for her own bizarre reasons." Tears began to pour down his face again. "I may not have loved her—or even liked her, but I'm really sorry she's dead, and I can't believe she'd do this. I feel so responsible."

Regarding Bodhi sympathetically, Officer Everts said, "If you don't mind me saying so, I think you might benefit from some grief counseling. A priest, a psychologist... some professional who's used to this kind of thing. We can have a social worker call you with a recommendation if you need one."

Bodhi nodded absently. It wasn't even apparent whether the cop's words penetrated his anguish.

"Anyway, the coroner's report ought to be available in a few days unless they decide to run a toxicology study on the body. Those can take from four to six weeks, I'm sorry to say."

Officer Prue added, "There was no purse or phone in the car, and obviously she didn't leave them here. Can you tell us whether she had family anywhere? We'll need to notify them as soon as possible."

Rousing himself a little, Bodhi looked thoughtful for a moment and then answered, "All I know is she supposedly has an aunt who lives in London, and she came from Arizona. She never mentioned any family to me, and you'd think she would have while she was planning our sham of a wedding. I tried to have as little contact with her as possible after meeting her, and really, the only conversations I had with her after our initial meeting were to tell her to stop the stupid lies and quit planning for a wedding that was never going to happen. She carried on as if I'd never said a word and sent me daily updates about the plans and sent crazy invitations to everyone I worked with. It was creepy and scary, actually. When she got here, I could never get any information about a family from her."

Eventually the police left. Cooper and Ivy looked at each other and had one of their silent conversations that resulted in both of them calling their assistants to report taking a few personal days rather than leaving Bodhi alone with his nightmare. That he needed their company was painfully obvious.

Bodhi spent a lot of time on the couch. His former bedroom seemed like kryptonite, and he wasn't ready to join Ivy and Cooper. He just felt dead inside. After a few days of this level of inactivity and wallowing in his misery, however, he got up one morning and announced, "I'm going to go to the morgue." No record of Blair Hendrix appeared in any search for family in Arizona or London, according to the police, and Blair's body was still awaiting burial instructions.

"We'll go with you," Ivy said firmly.

"I'll drive," offered Cooper.

A couple of hours later, Bodhi met with the coroner and announced, "I'll take care of them."

"Sir? I'm afraid I don't understand," the coroner answered.

"The bodies. They're my responsibility. I'll bury them." The baby girl was so real to Bodhi he thought of her as a separate person from Blair even in utero.

Looking alarmed, the coroner asked, "Was there someone with her when she jumped? Only one body was recovered, and it was my understanding that her suicide was witnessed by several people. No one reported another jumper."

Bodhi shielded his eyes for a moment and explained with a broken voice, "No,,, I mean the baby."

"She was holding a baby? I'm sure you're mistaken, sir. That would have made climbing over the bird spikes and up onto the wall extremely difficult. Perhaps she left the baby in someone's care before going to the bridge."

"No!" Bodhi insisted. "She was pregnant with my baby."

The lights went on in the coroner's eyes, and he said gently, "I'm quite certain you're mistaken. The autopsy showed there was no baby. In fact, I doubt she could have conceived in her condition."

Completely taken aback, Bodhi asked, "What condition?"

"She must have been in tremendous pain, sir. You didn't know she was suffering from stage four pancreatic cancer?"

Suddenly everything went fuzzy for Bodhi, and his knees gave out on him. Cooper grabbed for him before he fell. He led Bodhi to a nearby chair and asked, "Can we get him some water, please?"

An assistant ran and produced a bottle from somewhere that Bodhi accepted absently as he whispered, "Sonofabitch."

"I think that about covers it," Ivy said sympathetically.

Bodhi processed in silence for a long time. Finally, he sighed. "Thank God there was no baby after all. It's sad, in a way, but a hell of a lot less sad than the baby dying because she was a girl. That woman was completely off her rocker." With his voice growing in volume, he asked, "Why the charade, though?" He looked at his friends with utter disbelief.

"We may never know," Ivy mused. "Are you still going to take care of the... remains?"

"Well, someone has to, I guess." He looked questioningly at the coroner.

"If you are comfortable with that," the coroner replied. "If you choose not to make arrangements, the body will be held in storage for a year and then cremated if no one related to her shows up to take responsibility."

"I'll do it. She may have been awful and messed up, but no one deserves to be held in storage."

* * *

Bodhi had to sign a lot of documents and make a bunch of calls to organize Blair's final arrangements. At least it kept him busy for a couple of days, and he didn't have a lot of time to dwell on his guilt and annoyance. But those emotions crept in anyway as he ran out of busy work and had to confront his emotions.

Each evening, Ivy and Cooper did their best to pull Bodhi out of his funk, but he seemed terribly withdrawn. Cooper tried to get Bodhi to go surfing, and Ivy made sure Bodhi had lots of tasty things to eat. Their efforts went unnoticed, unfortunately. Bodhi seemed to prefer brooding. They kept an eye on him—making sure he didn't end up drinking to excess, but Bodhi didn't seem interested in that either. He just moped and thought about his life.

Blair hadn't packed any personal items that gave them a clue to her origins or her family, so there was nothing they wanted to keep in case anyone was ever found.

While helping Bodhi pack up Blair's belongings, Ivy pointed out, "This stuff is all knock-off designer junk. Not one thing is what it's supposed to be. She really was a fraud through and through, wasn't she?" Nevertheless, they donated every last item to charity—even the fake designer luggage.

Finally, the three of them had their own personal memorial at home, toasting one last time to Blair's sorry memory. There hadn't been anyone else to invite or notify as far as they knew. During their somber acknowledgment, the Telophase Cremation Society took her ashes out to sea for a water burial in the Pacific Ocean.

Chapter Seventeen

Bodhi thought he ought to be feeling himself returning to normal, but although the idea of having lost a child no longer haunted him, he still felt seething anger toward Blair for all she'd put him through. On top of that, he felt guilty for being so angry at someone who was clearly unhinged, extremely sick, and probably didn't know what to do with herself. *What was it*, he wondered daily, *that drew Blair to me? Why was she so fixated on me? Am I just expecting a logical answer when one doesn't exist? The woman was clearly not well mentally.*

After their memorial of sorts, Ivy and Cooper tried giving him space at first and then they tried their best to cheer up Bodhi with interesting conversation, but he was like a shadow of his former self. Bodhi had always taken pride in his appearance, but now he stopped shaving, and combing his hair seemed like an inconvenience. At least he showered regularly. Often, he glared at the television all night and slept on the couch at weird hours. They attempted to get him out to the beach or out for a run, but he never seemed to have the energy.

Ivy even asked Bodhi if he'd like to teach her how to surf. He just shrugged and said, "Maybe. But not today." Then he would ask the questions he repeated over and over. "Why did she have to target me? How did I miss that she was so sick? Why was it so important to lie to me? What kind of a sick-o pretends to be having your baby just to get health insurance? She knew I'd find out eventually! Didn't she care?" And on and on it went. One of his favorites seemed to be, "How could I have been so stupid?"

Finally, Ivy and Cooper were sick and tired of Bodhi moping around looking angry all the time and decided to stage something of an intervention—their own style. One night after dinner, they got on either side of him, grasped him firmly by the arms, and took charge as they escorted him down the hall.

"You need this, Bodhi," ordered Ivy. "Cooper and I want to raise your spirits in the best way possible. It's for your own good." She winked at him, and for the first time in what seemed like forever, Bodhi felt something inside himself coming to life. Or maybe it was just the beginnings of a boner.

Cooper shoved Bodhi down on the bed and unceremoniously began to remove his buddy's clothes. Bodhi got an amused expression on his face as Ivy started removing her own clothing next to him.

"We'll take care of you, Bodhi. You don't need to do anything," she purred as Bodhi ogled her glorious tits. He loved those tits. She began to stroke his body and massage his muscles as Cooper shucked off his clothes.

"We're going to make you feel so good," she crooned as she stroked his growing erection. She sat on one side of Bodhi, and Cooper sat on the other. They used their hands on him together and separately. As she leaned in to kiss his belly, Cooper kissed Bodhi on the mouth. Then they traded places with their mouths.

Cooper looked at Ivy, and they both scooted down to where they could use their mouths together on Bodhi's now rigid dick. They licked it up and down, dueling for position as they mixed kissing each other with licking Bodhi. Ivy began to use her tongue to stroke the base of his shaft as Cooper engulfed the head with his mouth.

Bodhi let out a rasping growl of appreciation. *Why have I been trying to deny myself this pleasure?* he asked himself. *How stupid.* He reached down to stroke the heads of the two people most dear to him in his life. He didn't want to feel like a pity fuck, but the fact that they took over was surprisingly gratifying and undeniably arousing. *Maybe I don't always have to take charge. I really kind of like this for a change.*

"Bodhi?" Ivy asked, blinking up at him. "We have an idea of something that both Cooper and I love, but you and I never did it together. Are you game for an experiment? We can do to you what Cooper loves me to do to him, only this way it will be better."

Bodhi's level of arousal was reaching a colossal high, so he croaked out, "Sure. Do whatever it is." He didn't miss that his lovers smiled knowingly at each other and looked eager.

Cooper reached around and came back with a bottle of lube and a strange-looking dildo. Bodhi felt his insides turn into mush at the sight of it.

"Ivy likes the dick end, and I like the plug end. You can try both if you want. I can't wait to use this on you," Cooper explained softly. His eyes bore into Bodhi's with shining intensity. He greased up the glass plug end first and commanded Bodhi, "Raise your knees and open your legs for us."

Ivy leaned back down and sucked the head of Bodhi's erection into her mouth. He let out a long, satisfied moan as he felt the silky warmth of her tongue and lips. She stroked up and down in time with her sucking.

Cooper, in the meantime, gently shoved Bodhi's legs apart and lifted his balls. He stroked a lubed finger around and around Bodhi's puckered hole, making Bodhi tighten up his muscles in surprise. After the lube was spread around, Cooper lightly pushed against the opening with the tip of his finger.

Bodhi gasped at this sensation that was completely foreign and yet exciting to him. His breathing sped up as Cooper exerted more pressure on his asshole. Then he felt the tip of

Cooper's finger entering him, and Bodhi's eyes slammed shut as he muttered, "Fuck." And then, "Don't stop."

He relished the feel of Ivy playing with his titanium erection while Cooper eased his finger in and out of Bodhi's opening. Nothing could have prepared him for the strength of the sensations that swept through his tense body.

"Relax your muscles," ordered Cooper. And as he felt Bodhi do so, he dribbled a little more lube onto his fingers and probed Bodhi now with two digits at the same time. Cooper smiled as Bodhi gasped and writhed. He stroked in and out with gentle pressure until he could feel the muscles softening. At that point, he said, "I'm going to use the plug now."

Bodhi's eyes flew open, and he watched with rapt attention as Cooper slicked the glass plug end with more lube. Cooper lowered it between Bodhi's legs and pushed.

With a huge intake of breath, Bodhi tried to relax his anal muscles. He'd thought about what this might feel like, but only in vague terms. He kept his eyes on Cooper's serious expression. Cooper seemed to be holding back—not wanting to hurt Bodhi. Suddenly the need to be filled overtook Bodhi with a vengeance and he shoved himself against the toy in Cooper's hand. A slash of pain ripped through his body with alarming speed and intensity, radiating out from his core to his extremities, and his face went rigid as his jaw dropped and his eyes bugged. The pain was so all-encompassing, he felt reborn by it as it morphed into exquisite pleasure. The sensation drove away everything in his mind except the rhapsody of his exhilaration.

"Relax, man. Take it slow and it won't hurt," Cooper explained softly. He started to pull away with the toy.

"Don't stop!" Bodhi ordered. "Fuck me with it, Cooper!"

Cooper's expression went from concern to delight, and Ivy chuckled as she kept sucking and stroking Bodhi's dick.

Cooper thrust the plug all the way to the hilt and then began manipulating it in and out incrementally.

Bodhi let out a long moan and asked in a choked voice, "Can you try the other end? I need more."

Cooper removed the plug, causing Bodhi to cry out as the widest part breached his sphincter. He watched avidly as Cooper now greased up the longer, phallic end of the toy. It was a beautiful piece of erotic art with a raised blue accent that swirled around a clear cylinder of glass. The entire piece measured about ten inches in length with a barrier about two-thirds the way down that separated the two elements.

Cooper placed the phallus against Bodhi's hole and gently pushed it inside. This time Bodhi saw stars when he felt its length penetrating him more deeply than the plug end had done. He growled in pleasure when it bumped against his prostate and moaned when Cooper twisted it as he pumped the toy in and out. The textured edges played against Bodhi's sensitive opening, and each time it hit his prostate, he wanted to explode with ecstasy. He held back with colossal effort.

Bodhi had never dreamed of sensations this intense—this pleasurable. His dick was on fire with the delight of Ivy's mouth and her hands stroking him, and his butt had never felt anything like what Cooper was doing to him. His breathing sped up, and his body broke out into a sweat as the sensations built and built to a crescendo that was inevitable and earth-shattering. Cooper gently squeezed Bodhi's balls and moved the dildo with more and more speed and determination until Bodhi roared out, "Fuck me! Ohhh ahhh..."

Ivy swallowed Bodhi's release, sucking until she finally felt him softening. She sat back and took in Bodhi's incredulous look as she gave him a knowing smile. "Welcome back, Bodhi," she whispered.

Bodhi lay panting for a moment and then got a gleam in his eye. "Ivy, I want to watch Cooper fuck you now. Lie back."

He noticed Cooper's impressive erection was already oozing precum. Bodhi sat up and made room for Ivy to lie down in the middle of the large bed. Before he did anything else, however, he grasped Cooper in his hand and licked the shining head of his dick.

Cooper moaned and closed his eyes as Bodhi sucked him into his mouth. Bodhi's tongue swirled around Cooper's sensitive head over and over before pulling off with a pop.

As soon as Ivy positioned herself, Bodhi leaned in to kiss her voraciously. He could still taste Cooper's saltiness, and now it was mixed with the flavor of his own ejaculate in Ivy's mouth. An unholy desire to rut and conquer overtook Bodhi. He tore his lips from Ivy's and locked them onto a somewhat startled Cooper's mouth. Their tongues dueled and their teeth nipped at each other's lips.

Bodhi pulled away with a leer and ordered, "Fuck Ivy, Coop. I need to watch." He looked at Ivy and commanded her, "Open your legs for him now."

As Cooper fed his length into Ivy's eager glistening cunt, Bodhi reached for the bottle of lube. He squirted a healthy dose of it into his hand and proceeded to grease up both hands with it. Then he snaked one hand beneath where the two lovers were joined and began to massage Ivy's bottom. She moaned as he timed his motions with Cooper's thrusts in and out of her. Then he plunged his index finger into her as she cried out, "Yes!"

His other hand, also generously lubed, went to Cooper's backside, and Bodhi repeated the same motions on his buddy as he had on Ivy. Gently at first, and then with greater pressure, he pushed his index finger into Cooper. The angle was awkward, but Bodhi had the sensation of being puppet master as he attempted to control their motions together. Cooper had yet to react to Bodhi, so Bodhi rammed a second finger into

Cooper's hole, and his friend finally cried out as his head went back and his eyes closed.

"Ohmygod," breathed Cooper. "That feels amazing. Keep going, Bodhi." He looked down at Ivy whose expression was one of rapture and wonder, and he couldn't resist kissing the daylights out of her. Cooper's kiss had to end, however, as the pleasure of feeling her warmth encompassing his dick and Bodhi's thrusts into his ass overtook his senses. He needed to breathe.

"Fuck her, Coop. Hard!" He shoved more brutally into Cooper, faster and faster as he drove their coupling. "She likes it hard, don't you, baby?" He looked at Ivy's face that seemed transported somewhere unattainable—she was so lost in her own pleasure. Bodhi smirked and chuckled at how beautifully they responded to him. Then he ordered, "Rub your clit, Ivy. Make yourself come all over Cooper so I can see it."

The place where they were joined was now a frenzy of hands and genitals—all shoving and stroking. The room filled with gasps and groans. Bodhi thought the sound was more beautiful than any symphony ever written, and he doubled his efforts. It seemed like an eternity of pleasure, but it was actually only minutes before Ivy's body stiffened and she began to buck and holler with her orgasm.

Seeing this, Cooper couldn't resist letting go as well. He squeezed his ass cheeks together, clamping down on Bodhi's hand as Cooper thrust and moaned with his own release.

They all collapsed in a heap when it was over. Matching satisfied grins graced each of their faces. Their chests rose and fell as their breathing gradually went back to normal.

Finally, Ivy spoke up. "I don't know about you guys, but I need a shower." Then she added, "That was incredible."

Chapter Eighteen

The next morning, Cooper and Bodhi made plans to go surfing together after Cooper got home from work. Everyone took this as a positive sign that Bodhi was finally returning to himself.

A couple of hours after Cooper and Ivy left, Bodhi was surfing the net rather than the waves when his phone rang. The caller ID was the Maylor-Essex Clinic. That sounded vaguely familiar, but he didn't know why. With a shrug, he answered.

"Hello, this is Dr. Marjorie Finch. Is this Bodhi Monaghan?"

"Yes."

Dr. Finch let out what sounded like a relieved sigh and continued, "Oh good. I'm sorry to bother you, but I've been trying to reach your wife for a while, and she hasn't returned any of my calls. I've left her several urgent messages. Is she all right?"

Frowning confusedly, Bodhi answered, "I think you're mistaken. I'm not married."

"Wh...? Um, you're not married to a woman named Blair Henry?"

Bodhi covered his eyes for a moment and tried to control his breathing. "If you're talking about Blair *Hendrix*, we're not married. I don't know a Blair Henry."

"Well, this is terribly confusing. Tall? Blonde? Recently relocated from London?"

"That's Blair alright. She told me her last name was Hendrix."

"Is Blair... whatever-her-last-name-is there? May I speak to her?"

"I'm afraid not. She's dead."

Dr. Finch gasped, "Oh no! So soon? I thought she had more time than that. Why wasn't I notified?"

"She committed suicide, I'm sorry to say." Bodhi cleared his throat finding it still difficult to talk about. "What did you want with her? She never mentioned you. No one knew you should have been notified."

"She never mentioned...? Oh, I'm so sorry for your loss, Mr. Monaghan. You must be devastated. She spoke about you in such glowing terms, and she was such a lovely young woman."

"Um, yeah. Thanks." Bodhi had no idea how to process this woman's concern, and it was one more example of Blair's weird fixation on him. And she apparently had the good doctor snowed about what a "lovely" person she was.

"I think perhaps it would be a good idea for us to speak face-to-face. I don't feel right about having this conversation over the phone. Do you have some time?"

Bodhi snorted and answered, "I have all the time in the world."

"Do you think you could come by my office today? I'm at the Maylor-Essex Clinic in the Oncology Department. Or, if you're too far away maybe we could meet somewhere." She told him the address.

"I'll be there in an hour," Bodhi said and went to shower, trim his unkempt beard, and make himself presentable. As he wolfed down a quick sandwich, he wondered what in the world she could have to say to him.

* * *

The clinic turned out to be an ultramodern, sprawling property just off the freeway, so it was easy to find. Now he realized why the name was familiar. He'd seen it on the side of the building for years as he'd driven by. He'd just never paid much attention to it.

Bodhi was shown into a cluttered office by an assistant, who immediately checked out his left hand for a ring and then gave him a look that seemed to waver alternately between flirtation and compassion. He figured she probably wondered if he had terminal cancer and was gauging her odds with him. He smiled politely and thanked her dismissively. No reason to get the woman's hopes up.

Dr. Finch rose from her seat and shook his hand. "May I offer you some coffee? Water?"

"A water would be great. Thanks." Bodhi sat down as she pulled a couple of bottles out of a small refrigerator behind her desk.

"So, I'm very sorry to inconvenience you, Mr. Monaghan…"

"Please, just call me Bodhi."

"Yes, right. Then you should call me Marjie." She gave him a pleasant smile. "Again, let me offer my sincere condolences for your tragic loss, Bodhi. I know you must have been gearing up to the inevitable with Blair anyway, but suicide is so difficult for the grieving survivors."

Bodhi took a chug of water and tried not to snort. "I need to set the record straight. Although I appreciate your compassion, I barely knew Blair. She showed up at my house claiming to be carrying my baby after a brief encounter that may or may not have actually happened. Apparently, I'd had too much to drink to remember sleeping with her but woke up to find her naked in my bed. I'm not saying it didn't happen—only that I have no recollection of it—which is odd. That's never happened to me before, and I hadn't had *that* much to drink. So anyway, I got her some decent health insurance because I wanted to make sure that if she had my baby, she had the best possible care. Then I planned to arrange for full custody because Blair was completely unhinged. I frankly couldn't stand the woman, and you have no idea what she's put me through over the past few months. I was sure she'd killed herself and my child for her own twisted reasons until I learned about her lack of pregnancy and advanced stage of cancer from the coroner." He paused and saw the effect his words had on the doctor and added, "That about sums it up. Oh—I should add that she jumped off the Coronado Bridge after she stole my car to get there."

"Oh!"

"Yeah, oh. So, you can see why I may have some lingering fucked-up feelings, but I'd hardly characterize myself by saying I'm her grieving lover. I'm sure-as-shit not her husband. This fixation she had on telling everyone I was married to her is just..." He closed his eyes and shook his head. "So, what is it you wanted with Blair? You were trying to call her? Her phone has never been recovered and neither has her purse with her ID in it."

"Blair came to see me not too long ago and I had to turn her down for a special clinical trial she desperately wanted to be included in."

"That must have been the day she poisoned me so I couldn't accompany her to her so-called OB-GYN appointment."

Marjie gasped, "Poisoned you?"

"Yeah, just a tasty dollop of ipecac in my coffee. It's quite the way to start the day," he said with a grim expression. "Fuckin' bitch," he muttered under his breath.

"What a bitch!" exclaimed the doctor over his muttering. "Excuse me." Her hand flew to cover her mouth, and she had an embarrassed expression.

They stared at each other a beat and then she dropped her hand and continued, "Blair thought that if she had a robust health insurance plan the trial would accept her, but I made it clear that insurance companies do *not* cover experimental procedures. I'm sorry if she tricked you into paying for coverage for her, especially on a fool's errand. She finally seemed to accept the insurance limitation and told me that her husband—I assume she meant you because she filled out forms with your name and phone number on them—would be more than willing and financially able to foot the bill. She was rather poetic about how much you loved her and how devastated you'd be if she passed away. She went on and on about how optimistic and excited you were for her to have a spot in the program. I thought that was admirable and frankly wondered why you weren't with her, but I had to let her know that her cancer was far too advanced to be accepted into the program. That was a hard conversation to have, believe me. We here at the clinic didn't think it would be fair to deprive another individual of the real chance of survival if she took up one of the limited spots. It sounds cold-hearted, I know, but we sometimes have to make very tough decisions."

"It's all quite understandable. I'm sorry she tried to dupe you and yanked on your heartstrings to get what she wanted. But... why were you trying to get hold of Blair so badly if you'd already turned her down?"

With a disparaging look, Marjie explained, "We have a drug that's just become available that I thought would alleviate some of her terrible pain and give her a bit more energy during the time she had left. Even though she wasn't admitted into the program, she was still under my care. I'm frankly amazed at how well she was getting around as it was, but it would have made her final weeks or months much more tolerable. I'm so sorry I was too late reaching out to her."

Bodhi nodded. He felt guilty for thinking Blair was lazy and unhelpful. The woman had been dealing with a lot. "I would have done anything to save our baby. I'm just glad there wasn't one that she... you know."

"I'm so sorry. That must have been a terrible experience for you," she offered with eyes full of compassion. It made Bodhi realize how often she had to deal with grieving loved ones.

Thinking it was time to be practical, he said, "So far no one has been able to locate any relatives, and she wouldn't ever tell me anything about her family. Did Blair give you any information? Family history? Where they live—that kind of thing? They ought to be informed."

She looked thoughtfully at her computer screen and tapped a few keys. Bodhi watched as her eyes scanned the monitor. "It says here her next of kin and the responsible party is you. Under the category for her father, it says, 'none' and for her mother it lists a Lauren Henry in Chuckwalla, Arizona. Does that help?"

Bodhi nodded. "More than I had before."

"There's no address or phone number listed, I'm sorry to say."

"Well, it's a start. People aren't all that hard to find when you have the right name, and it sounds like a small town. Thank you. Oh, I have one more question for you," he added. "How did Blair find you and your program? She had to have known about it before she arrived in California."

"Yes, she was a referral from a friend of mine in London. We went to med school together. His name is Stanley Burroughs, and he's also an oncologist. He moved there when his wife wanted to go back to England."

"I see. Okay, well, maybe Stanley can shed a little more light on Blair for me. It hardly matters at this point, but I am curious."

"Bodhi, I'm sorry, but something just dawned on me. You said it was uncharacteristic behavior for you to drink to such excess that you forgot certain... activities. Is it possible that

Blair also drugged you the night you supposedly had sex with her? Maybe you don't remember it because you were under the influence of more than alcohol."

Bodhi squinted his eyes and thought back to that night so long ago. And then the light went on. "How long does it take a date rape drug to take effect on someone? I left my beer with Blair and hit the loo before we headed out. It was a short walk back to my place, and I remember pretty much collapsing once we got there. Everything else is a blur. I chalked it up to drinking, no food, and very little sleep."

"If you swallowed some Rohypnol, it would take anywhere from fifteen to thirty minutes to make you drowsy. It sounds to me as if that's a distinct possibility."

"Sonofabitch! That woman was bad news from the get-go. I can't believe her."

"Why do you think she would do that?"

Bodhi turned to look out the window and tried to gather his thoughts. "She seemed to want someone to take care of her pretty desperately, and she got the idea that I was wealthy. I guess she thought she could trap me into marrying her and used every crazy trick in her arsenal to get there." He shook his head and looked down. "I'm really sorry she felt she had to commit suicide. My heart goes out to anyone who's that troubled. I'm just equally sorry, however, that I was roped into her drama. She's messed up my life as well as those of my close friends. And now someone needs to find that mother of hers and let her know. I guess that someone ought to be me."

"You're a good man, Bodhi. I hope you don't mind my saying that I think you'll make some nice woman very happy someday."

Bodhi scoffed lightly and answered, "Yeah, well... my track record so far has been pretty bad." He tried to look business-like and asked, "So... Lauren Henry in Chuckwalla, you say? Sounds... um... colorful."

Smiling, Marjie said, "I wish I had more to go on for you, but that's all the information I have. Like you say, though, it can't be too big of a town."

Bodhi turned to leave, and Marjie stood to follow him to the door. She shook his hand and as he opened the door, she said, "It was a pleasure meeting you, Bodhi. Good luck with everything. I hope you get some answers and find what you're looking for. I'm sorry for everything that's happened."

"Sure. Thanks. It was nice meeting you too." He gave the doctor one of his killer smiles and strode out. He didn't notice the assistant eyeballing him as he went for his phone and hastily called Cooper. As he walked by her desk, he said into the phone, "Hey, Coop. I need some big waves to clear my head after the day I've had, so I'm thinking La Jolla. I'll head over early and see you at Windansea whenever you can get there. I hope that's okay with you. Bye." It was obvious he was leaving a message for someone as he clicked off before waiting for a response.

The assistant smiled to herself as she realized this wasn't some terminally ill man. *Windansea Beach isn't too far from where I live in Pacific Beach. Maybe the sunset there will be spectacular tonight. It's worth checking out. He looks like a man who might need some comfort.*

Chapter Nineteen

Once Bodhi changed and made it over to La Jolla, found a place to park, and trekked down to Windansea with his board, he was tired of thinking. His thoughts were too loud. He yanked on his wetsuit and paddled for all he was worth out to the spot where the surfers all waited for the next swells. It wasn't too congested with tourists for a change, so that was a bonus. He found a spot to wait that wasn't crowding anyone. Years of experience at this beach told him his choice was a good one. He knew which way these waves tended to break.

He felt his mind cooling and relaxing as he took the soothing ocean air into his lungs. The contrast of the hot sun and cold water felt like home. *How did I ever think I could give this up for good?* he wondered for the hundredth time to himself. *What was I thinking?*

Bodhi rode a couple of waves in and then went back out immediately, only to discover that the crowd was growing. People were leaving their drab jobs in fluorescent-lit cubicles and heading out to the sunshine and surf while it was still light. But from the looks of things, there were quite a few would-be surfers who should have chosen a calmer beach. Windansea was known for tall waves that broke quickly and with dramatic power. "Kooks" routinely wiped out badly when they didn't know what they were doing, and he knew he'd have to look out for them.

Bodhi let a couple of wave sets go by and watched the shoreline for Cooper. He wasn't sure what time it was, but judging by the angle of the sun, it had to be past closing time at the law office by now. Thinking about Cooper and Ivy made him smile finally. He had such an amazing sexual rapport with them—and it was so unexpected. He had to amend that thought. It was unexpected that he'd find it with them *together*. He knew he and Ivy had had a great sex life before he screwed up everyone's life by leaving. Just thinking about what the three of them had gotten up to together was making him horny. *Maybe tonight we can try some more new things.*

With that happy thought, Bodhi turned and saw the evidence of a great wave building up behind him. He paddled into position. Just as he stood up on his board, some gigantic lunatic came from out of nowhere and cut him off. Bodhi tried to back off, but he was too far committed with the wave. The jerk in front of him panicked and wiped out right in Bodhi's way, and immediately Bodhi saw that the kook had forgotten to do up his ankle leash for the board. The guy went one way, and the board another, flying up in the air and crashing into Bodhi's leg, sweeping him from his board. A slash of pain cut through his shin, and Bodhi was swallowed up by the breaking wave. Fortunately for him, he and his own board remained tethered.

What felt like a few tons of water pounded down on him, keeping him submerged for way longer than was comfortable. His board yanked on him as he tried to control himself. Water churned around him, and his lungs began to burn. He hated the feeling of helplessness, and the pain in his shin was awful.

Finally, Bodhi's head broke the surface of the water as he gasped for air and then bellowed, "Fuck!" Looking around in a panic, he tried to locate the nitwit who'd caused the problem, thinking that it was highly possible the asshole had drowned after that stupid stunt. However, he caught sight of the guy about thirty feet away swimming and then running through the shallow water toward his board as it washed ashore. The bonehead grabbed it and kept running, never once looking back to apologize or assess the damage he'd done to a fellow surfer.

Bodhi limped his way back to the beach and was immediately assaulted by a woman who grabbed his arm as if to help him walk. The pain burning through his leg was so intense, he barely registered her. All he thought was, *I hope this is just salt water in the wound and nothing more serious. It stings like a motherfucker.*

Finally, he realized that the woman was speaking to him as if she knew him. That was weird. "Bodhi? Are you okay?" she asked in a rapid-fire voice. "I saw what happened out there. I was watching you. That was pretty rude of that guy. Come and sit down over here. I have a big blanket where you can get comfortable." She led him to a gaudy, flowery thing that was as wide as a bed where he flopped down and lay on his back. He needed to catch his breath.

Bodhi squinted curiously at the woman, thinking she looked a little like Blair. She had long blonde hair and, except for her fake boobs, was just about as curvaceous as a ten-year-old boy with one of those straight up-and-down, skinny bodies. She apparently thought wearing the tiniest bikini ever invented was a good idea, though to Bodhi it just looked sleazy. With the sun behind her, he couldn't get a good look at her face. "Sorry, do I know you?" he asked.

"Oh, yeah. I'm Dr. Finch's assistant. I met you today at the clinic. Can I get you something for your leg? It's bleeding."

Oh yeah. The eager assistant, Bodhi sighed to himself. "Thanks, but I'll be okay."

Not taking the hint, she dropped to the blanket next to him, announcing perkily, "I'm Tabitha."

What is it with these skinny blonde chicks? "Hi." Bodhi closed his eyes again trying to ignore both her and the pain in his leg.

"You're bleeding pretty badly, Bodhi. You might even need stitches." She knelt and leaned over him to assess the damage to his calf, and Bodhi could feel the unwelcome heat of her body as she moved way too close to him for comfort. Her boobs were in danger of spilling out, and he realized her bikini bottom was barely more than a string that left her entire butt exposed. He might have enjoyed seeing something like this on Ivy—privately—but not in public on *this* woman.

"I'll be fine." He had no idea if he'd actually be fine—he just wanted her to get the fuck away from him. Bodhi sat up and collided with her upper body, causing him to have to grab her so she didn't land in his lap. The last thing he wanted was for her to face-plant on his junk.

Just then Bodhi heard a much more welcome voice on his other side. "Are we interrupting something?" asked Cooper with a tiny bit of an edge to his voice. "Who's your friend, Bodhi?"

Bodhi's head whipped around to see not just Cooper, but also Ivy standing there. His outlook on life suddenly improved immeasurably. "Hey!" he cried happily as he jumped to his feet and then grimaced with the pain.

Looking down, Ivy exclaimed, "Bodhi! You're bleeding all over the place. Did a shark bite you or something?" She was only half kidding as she slanted her eyes toward Tabitha.

Bodhi looked down at his leg finally and assessed the gash that started just below his knee. He had to agree with Tabitha that it might benefit from a few stitches—a couple of butter-fly bandages at the very least and some antibiotic ointment. "I guess I ought to hit the drugstore and fix this up." He looked at Cooper and added, "I'm sorry. I probably shouldn't go out and surf with you now. Some asshole newb got in my way and lost his board. He's lucky I didn't run over him and kill the jerk by accident. The board flipped into me, and I caught the fin with my leg. Too bad I wasn't wearing my long wetsuit. It may have protected me from getting sliced open."

"Or it would have sliced through the wetsuit and your leg," observed Ivy.

"Yeah, maybe," agree Bodhi. He looked curiously at Ivy and asked, "It's great to see you, but why are you here? I was just planning to surf with Cooper a while and then head home." He was sorry to realize that Tabitha had also stood up and was inching toward him as though to take his arm. He stepped closer to his friends before she could latch on.

"We thought it would be fun to take you out to dinner after this somewhere in La Jolla, so I was just going to relax until you guys were done. We brought you clothes to change into, but now I think we need to get you fixed up before going any-where." She eyed Tabitha and then raised an eyebrow at Bodhi.

"I'm free tonight," Tabitha piped up in a chirpy voice that grated on Bodhi's ears. She batted her eyelashes at him as he stared at her. She turned to Cooper and said, "Hi, I'm Tabitha!" Squinting at him for a moment she asked, "Wait, don't I know you?" Then she gasped and frowned, "I remember you. You're that lawyer. I thought we had something going on, and then you never called me!"

Bodhi turned his attention to his friends and saw Cooper's jaw clench and Ivy's eyes look sad. Without any further thought, he grabbed Ivy and gave her a long, passionate kiss. As he kissed Ivy, he reached out to Cooper and grabbed his arm, drawing him closer to them. He quit kissing Ivy and immediately locked lips with Cooper. He felt Cooper's body stiffen and then relax into the kiss, but when he pulled back, Cooper's slack-jawed expression was one of total disbelief.

After blinking for a beat, Cooper whispered, "PDA on a public beach? Really?"

Bodhi winked at Cooper and then turned to Tabitha asking casually, "Are you into orgies?"

Tabitha's face turned fifty shades of red and she cleared her throat. Then nothing came out. She was apparently speechless. Bodhi's ears liked that idea.

"Yeah, it's okay, we don't really share anyway. Just thought I'd be polite," he added with a smirk and a small shrug. Turning to Ivy and Cooper, he said, "Let's hit the drugstore and then go grab some takeout. I'd rather *eat* at home." He winked at Ivy. "If you know what I mean."

Screwing up her courage, Tabitha said in a shaky voice, "Um... maybe I could..."

"No, you couldn't," Ivy stated in a no-nonsense voice. "They're both mine. Let's go, guys." She waited for Bodhi to grab his board and latched onto his free hand, intending to lead the two men away from Tabitha.

Before walking away, Bodhi politely thanked Tabitha for trying to help him. Once they were out of earshot he chuckled. "Ivy, I love it that you got all cavewoman possessive about your men."

"Ugh. How could you stand that... person—with her fake tan and her fake boobs and her fake hair? And that bikini she must have made out of dental floss? *Look at me! Look at me!* What a prize."

"Hey, I had nothing to do with it. She glommed onto me. I think she's another fortune hunter. Too bad I'm not as rich as all of these women seem to think I am."

"Oh, I think they see more than your wallet," observed Cooper with a smile. He seemed to be relaxing now that they were away from Tabitha's clutches. He hadn't wanted to think of Bodhi out on his own picking up random women.

"And you too, Cooper," Ivy went on peevishly as if Bodhi hadn't said a thing. "You went out with her? She obviously recognized you." She gave a tiny shudder.

"I may have hooked up with her once back in my lonely, single days before you stole my heart and made me a monogamous man. What was her name? Tammy? Tally?" He looked at Bodhi.

"Something like that." Bodhi shrugged. "And who says you're monogamous? I think the word 'polyamorous' fits better. Anyway, she's probably okay—just looking for some fun. I'm sorry I bled all over her bedspread. She was nice enough to try to help me, and I think I shocked her." He laughed. "I met her earlier today and I'd already forgotten her."

They found Bodhi's car and got him cleaned up enough to drive, agreeing to meet over at the closest drugstore. Ivy called in an order for their food so they could get it on the way home.

Chapter Twenty

Back at home, they patched up Bodhi's leg with butterfly bandages and then sat down to a delicious dinner. Several times Cooper asked if he could drive Bodhi to the ER to have his leg stitched up properly, but each time, Bodhi brushed him off, saying, "It's just a big scratch," or "I'll be fine." Eventually Cooper gave up.

Ivy asked, "So, Bodhi, if we hadn't shown up, what were you planning to do with Miss Fakey-Fake?"

"I wasn't planning on doing anything with her. I just needed to sit down for a minute, and she was watching me and dragged me over to her dry blanket. I'm not interested in hooking up, you know," he eyed Ivy seriously. "I have all I can handle and more than enough to enjoy right here with the two of you." He paused. "That is, unless you're tired of having me in bed with you. I don't want to mess up your engagement. I also don't want to be booted out, so I'm in a rather precarious position with you right now."

"So, are you looking for some kind of commitment from us?" she asked.

Bodhi gave her a thoughtful look. "Commitment is a strong word."

"Well, duh. I seem to remember you were a real commitment-phobe a year or so ago. Are you ready to grow up?"

"Are you asking me to commit?"

"Does anyone care what I think?" interjected Cooper who looked amused and a little frustrated.

"Of course, we do," Bodhi answered for both of them.

Cooper looked from Bodhi to Ivy and said, "You both know I love you."

Bodhi chimed in, "And I do as well... love you both, I mean. Ivy?"

She narrowed her eyes at Bodhi and said, "I know I love Cooper. And I'm equally sure that I loved you before you smashed my heart into bits." Bodhi started to interrupt her, but she raised her hand to silence him. "You're definitely growing on me, Bodhi. I saw the way you treated Blair with kindness and generosity even while she was lying and manipulating you. It takes a good man to do what you did while you were helping her with what you thought was your baby. That impressed me. I can't say yet that I'm certain I'm in love with you, but I may be able to get there."

"What do I need to do?" he asked.

"Nothing specific. Just be your best self and I'll see if I can catch up. If you want to be a part of our relationship, we have to know we can trust you a hundred percent."

"Well, I'm relieved," Cooper sighed.

"Relieved?" asked Ivy.

"Yes. I have literally had nightmares that Bodhi would come sweeping back into town and I'd lose you to him. You loved him long before you loved me, and I worried I was a placeholder." He looked down as his face turned pink.

Ivy stood and went to Cooper. She crawled into his lap and whispered to him, "I won't stop loving you. Never worry about that." She nuzzled his neck. "But I love seeing the two of you together and it's beyond exciting to have you both to myself."

Cooper chuckled, "You little perv."

Ivy gave a belly laugh. "And proud of it!" Then she turned to Bodhi and said, "That was so freakin' hot when you kissed Cooper at the beach. What possessed you to do that?"

"I wanted to lose the barnacle and publicly stake my claim on the two best people I've ever known. Seriously, thank you for sticking by me during the shitstorm that's been going on. I would have been a mess by myself. I know I haven't always been good company, but having you near kept me sane."

"We're happy to be here for you, man," announced Cooper.

"Would you guys like to take a road trip with me this weekend?" Bodhi explained about getting a call from the clinic and finding where Blair's mother lived in Chuckwalla, Arizona. "I'm curious to meet the woman who raised Blair and to possibly understand why she was so messed up. She needs to know Blair is gone, so I guess I'm the one who needs to tell her."

"Sure," answered Cooper as he looked for assent from Ivy. "I'll drive. You might not want to drive a long way with that sore leg."

"I'll come along and keep you guys out of trouble," agreed Ivy with a giggle. She gave Cooper another smooch.

"Oh," added Bodhi, "I meant to tell you... the doctor I met today at the cancer clinic thinks it's highly likely that Blair roofied me, and that's why I had no recollection about that night. The doctor was also led to believe that I was madly in love with Blair and would do just about anything to save her life. Blair made me out to be some kind of tragic hero."

"Well," Ivy piped up, "in a sense, you are. You were in love with the baby, even if you weren't in love with Blair."

Bodhi cleared his throat with difficulty. "Yeah, you're right on that score. I had all of these amazing ideas of how to raise my son. It was going to be *perfect*, and then Blair said, 'It's not a boy.'" He shook his head, looking down. "It dawned on me later that she wasn't even lying then. She *should* have said, 'It's not a baby,' though, and I wouldn't have jumped to conclusions and fallen in love with my little pink tutu-ed ballerina with sparkles everywhere. I'd even mentally picked out the puppy we were going to get when she was old enough." Bodhi's voice cracked. "I thought having a little girl would be so awesome." He rose from the table. "Excuse me a moment." He walked out the back door wiping his eye and stood watching the tail-end of the sunset. He needed to compose himself.

Ivy looked at Cooper and exclaimed softly, "I think my heart just exploded a little."

"I know just what you mean," answered Cooper, and then he kissed her softly. "Our boy's been through a lot, and he's really made for love now that he's not afraid of it." He looked deeply into Ivy's dark eyes and asked, "Do you think you can love both of us at the same time? I know it's a big thing to ask."

"I'm pretty sure I can get there, but how would it work? Do you still want to marry me?"

"I definitely do because I want a life with you. But I also don't want to give up on Bodhi. It's strange, but it feels so right and complete with the three of us. I don't mean just in bed, although that's amazing, but all of it. It's like things are perfect and balanced that way, you know?"

Ivy nodded. "I do know, actually." She smiled sweetly at Cooper and said, "Let's go get our man and take him to bed. We can have some fun now and worry about the details later, I guess. He just needs to know his affection is safe with us."

"I love you," he whispered and kissed her softly.

Chapter Twenty-One

Bodhi chuckled when his two best friends grabbed him by the arms and coaxed him back indoors. *As if they have to prod*, he thought. *Hah!*

"Cooper and I were talking, and we want to try an experiment," Ivy began in her best businesswoman voice. "If you think you're ready for it," she added as they all sat down on the large bed.

"Well, you make it sound about as interesting as a seventh-grade science project," Bodhi laughed. "I can't wait."

Ivy blushed. "Um, sorry. I'll start over." She smiled and cleared her throat. "Cooper and I were talking about it while we were driving home, and he had to adjust his boner three times." Cooper burst out laughing, but she went on, "We want you guys to fuck. For real. I think seeing that would be the hottest thing in the world, and my panties are getting wet just thinking about it. One of you can do me while the other of you does whoever's fucking me. Better?"

"Okay," laughed Bodhi. "Who's the bologna in this sandwich?"

"*Now* who sounds like a seventh-grader?" Cooper asked as Ivy snorted softly. "But if I can vote first, I'd like to watch you do Ivy for a change, while I take your ass. Are you the man for the job?" He smirked at Bodhi.

"Hell yes!" Bodhi jumped up with only a small grimace and began shucking his clothes. "Come on, you two, don't just stare at my bologna."

"We thought it might take a little persuasion for you to agree to that," Cooper said, a bit wide-eyed. "I guess not."

"Just as long as I don't have to kneel on my wounded leg, I'm ready and willing," Bodhi answered cheerfully. "I've been hoping for this actually. Get your clothes off!" He waved his hands at them in a "get a move-on" gesture.

Ivy laughed and said, "I do love an eager participant."

Bodhi blinked at her for a second and added, "Well, that's a step in the right direction for your affection, then."

Ivy realized what she'd said and considered telling Bodhi it was just a figure of speech, but she thought better of it and let her comment stand. *Let the man think what he wants. It's good to see him happy. And besides, I do love him—I'm just not ready to tell him so*, she mused to herself.

After assessing the layout of the room as well as his limitations with his lacerated shin, Bodhi took charge—as usual—and directed Ivy to scoot to the edge of the bed. The bed frame held the thick mattress nice and high—just right for his purposes.

While Cooper busied himself with getting lube and a condom, Bodhi kissed Ivy passionately and then made his way southward to her beloved breasts. He sucked and played with one then the other as she purred with pleasure. Finally, he dove right in between her spread legs. Caressing each of her silky thighs with his lips, he made his way closer and closer to her luscious pink parts. He spent a moment stroking her with his fingers and then worked his finger inside her as she studied his expression. He slowly pumped his finger in and out and then bent down to lick her. He swirled his tongue around her clit until she began to moan and writhe, and then he sucked the nub into his mouth. Holding her gently between his teeth,

Bodhi began rapid licks and probes with his stiff tongue. The taste of Ivy was so beautifully female, and the hungry little noises she made had his dick as hard as a steel rod within seconds.

Bodhi was so caught up tasting and teasing Ivy, he was barely aware of Cooper, who'd come up behind him. Gradually, it registered that Cooper was kissing his neck and shoulders. He was fully aware of Cooper, however, when his friend began stroking Bodhi's ass cheeks. Bodhi almost combusted when Cooper began to rut against his ass crack with a huge erection. *This is it,* he told himself. *After this I'll never be able to claim I'm not bi.* Rather than worrying about it, however, the thought made him feel free.

As Bodhi pondered his sexuality, Ivy shuddered with her release. Her thrashing brought his attention back to her. Giving her a tiny eyebrow wiggle and a smile, he rose up and slammed his dick deep into her cunt. He groaned as her body gripped him tightly. It had been so long since he'd been inside her. He had missed this more than words could say.

As if she felt the same way, Ivy gasped. She moved her hips in time with his thrusts as she panted, "Yes, fuck me, Bodhi! Cooper, fuck Bodhi!" She had a rosy blush that spread from her cheeks right down to her nipples.

Grabbing for Bodhi's butt, Ivy held on. She pulled his cheeks apart for Cooper. Wasting no time at all, Cooper squirted lube on his finger and began to circle and probe Bodhi. First with one finger and then two, he finger-fucked Bodhi until he could see that Bodhi was relaxed enough for him.

Bodhi was in a state of bliss. Never had he been so aroused with his dick inside this woman, so hot and tight around him. He could feel the heat of Cooper's body behind him as Cooper slid his fingers in and out of Bodhi's eager hole. A shudder went through him at last when he felt the broad head of Cooper's cock push against him.

Just as when Cooper had probed him with the dildo, Bodhi was all too eager to feel something buried inside him, so he relaxed his ass muscles and pressed back toward Cooper quickly. He almost lost contact with Ivy in his haste, but he was quickly thrust forward again by Cooper. Cooper intended to gently feed himself into Bodhi's body, but he also shared Bodhi's impatience to breach the ring of muscles. Cooper latched his teeth onto the lobe of Bodhi's ear and with one, long, strong shove, he made his way past the sphincter.

Bodhi cried out like he'd been stabbed, but his nearly frightened-sounding holler morphed immediately into "Yes, fuck, yes!" Once again, the intense stab of pain quickly turned into unbelievable pleasure as Cooper rubbed against Bodhi's prostate.

Ivy's eyes nearly bulged out of their sockets as she took in the looks on Bodhi and Cooper's faces. Pure rapture. Neither man was able to keep his eyes open.

Cooper wrapped his arms around Bodhi's body and then slowly began to relax enough to pull back and thrust in again. "I can't believe I'm actually inside you," he whispered into the ear that now bore red teeth marks on its lobe. "You feel incredible. So tight!"

Bodhi's chest began to heave as he allowed Cooper to drive him forward and back—in and out of Ivy. His body and his mind were on complete sensation overload. Eventually, he had the foresight to reach down and manipulate Ivy's clit with his fingers as his best friend drilled into him from behind. The dildo he'd felt before had nothing on the warmth and size of Cooper's erection. Bodhi wanted to live right here, in this very instant, for the rest of his life. He thought he'd found heaven, nirvana, and total enlightenment in this moment and time. He never wanted it to end. His body, however, began to writhe with ecstasy. In no time—even though he tried to prolong it— he found himself spilling into Ivy who was thrashing against him with her second orgasm. As he bellowed out with his release, Cooper also let go and thundered against Bodhi's back as he came and came.

All movement finally ceased, and the only sound in the room for a while was a chorus of heavy breathing. Each was lost in their own blissful thoughts until nature—and gravity—took its course, and Cooper slid out of Bodhi's backside. He kissed Bodhi's back and then leaned around him to kiss Ivy. She appeared sex-drunk as she lay motionless with a satisfied grin on her face.

"Was it as good as you hoped?" Cooper asked her.

Her eyes opened slowly, and she purred, "Way better. You two guys are incredible that way."

"Bodhi? You okay?" he asked.

Bodhi's eyes were still closed, and gradually a grin spread across his face as well. "You need to be the bologna in the sandwich next time, Coop. You won't believe how incredible that is to get it from both sides at once." He shook his head. "Straight dudes don't know what they're missing," he chuckled.

"I can't wait," laughed Cooper as he gave Bodhi's ass a friendly swat and went to get rid of the condom.

Chapter Twenty-Two

Early the next morning, they loaded up the car with drinks and snacks and programmed Cooper's GPS for the town of Chuckwalla. It would take them about three hours to drive from Del Mar to Yuma, and then Chuckwalla was several miles northeast in the middle of the desert. The plan was to stay in Yuma for the night before heading back.

"I'll take the back seat so you two can have plenty of legroom in front," Ivy told them. She'd packed her Kindle and her laptop, not knowing how bored she'd be during the long car ride. But as she situated herself in the back seat, hooked up her seatbelt, and stowed her stuff, she looked around the interior of the car. Suddenly she went cold, and it had nothing to do with the car's air-conditioning.

Bodhi turned around to ask Ivy something and saw a tear streaking down her face. His smile disappeared as he demanded, "Ivy? What's wrong?"

"Don't back the car out yet, Cooper," she demanded with a sniff—ignoring Bodhi's question. "I've just decided to stay home after all." She grabbed her stuff, climbed out, slammed the door, and stomped away.

Cooper looked at Bodhi with a stunned look on his face and asked, "What's up with her all of a sudden?"

"No clue. Just a few minutes ago she was asking me if I liked to play silly long-car-ride games. We better go find out, though. I sure as hell don't want to leave her here while she's upset about something."

When the two men got back into the house, they found Ivy in the kitchen. She'd grabbed a bottle of water and was heading outside with it. Her eyes were red, and she was wiping her cheek with the back of her hand.

"Ivy, honey, what's going on?" Cooper asked.

Without looking at him, she snapped, "You guys just go and have your fun. I need some time alone to think."

"Think about what?" they asked simultaneously.

Ivy swirled around and glared at Cooper. "About why you have some woman's stuff in the back of your car!"

"Stuff?" he asked incredulously. "What are you talking about?" Cooper looked truly baffled at her remark, and Bodhi's jaw dropped.

"There's a purse and a scarf and maybe some other crap under the seat of your car. I can just imagine how *that* got there! You probably stashed it..."

"Why would I stash some stupid shit in my car?" Cooper demanded. "I don't even know what you're talking about."

Bodhi got a funny look on his face and disappeared into the garage. Within seconds he was back with the objects Ivy had seen. "I think this must be Blair's stuff," he explained. "She must have hidden it there before she drove to Coronado."

"Why?" asked Ivy.

"Who knows? She had so many loose screws, it's impossible to guess what might have made her do any of the things she did. But I'm going to look through this junk before we leave. Maybe we can find her mother more easily this way... if it is Blair's stuff." He glanced over at Cooper.

"Of course it's Blair's," fumed Cooper. "I don't have random women leaving their things in my car, and frankly, Ivy, I'm pretty disappointed in your lack of trust in me."

Ivy hung her head in embarrassment as Bodhi opened the purse. It was immediately obvious by the smell that the bag belonged to Blair.

"I'm sorry, Cooper. I reacted too quickly and without thinking," she said softly. "I know I can trust you." She looked up. "It was a knee-jerk reaction to a surprise, that's all. Please don't be mad at me. I feel like an idiot, but you have to admit, it looked pretty weird."

"Just have some faith, would you?" he implored. "We've talked about trust over and over, and yet you jumped to a pretty reckless conclusion at the first hint of trouble. Are you sure you're as committed to me as you say?"

Ivy's eyes looked so sad when she answered, "I promise I trust you. I'm so sorry."

Cooper looked uncertain. And peeved. Ivy went to him and snuggled into his chest as she murmured her hopeful assurances to him.

In the meantime, Bodhi removed the contents of Blair's purse and laid them out on the kitchen table. There was a phone that had run out of juice, a makeup bag—the source of the perfume smell—a hairbrush, and a wallet. The wallet produced three dollars, a few coins, the card for the insurance Bodhi had paid for, and an expired Arizona driver's license that identified her as Blair Henry. The address on the license was 635 Saguaro Road, Chuckwalla, Arizona. In the outside zippered pocket of the purse, he found her US passport. That document identified her as Blair Hendrix, with a London address.

Rooting into the inside pocket of the purse, Bodhi whispered, "Well, look at this!" as he pulled out a diamond ring, a heavy gold bracelet, and a matching gold chain with a beautiful pendant attached to it. The pendant was in the shape of a fanciful bird and bore several precious stones set in an intricate design. It was certainly nothing he'd ever seen Blair wear and, as beautiful as it was, it seemed too old-fashioned for her taste. He couldn't help wonder if she'd stolen it from someone. *I wouldn't put it past her*, he thought.

Bodhi grabbed his laptop and typed the London address into a Google search. The answer was immediate: No such address was found. "I wonder if the passport is even authentic," he wondered out loud. "That woman was a real piece of work." He did the same thing with the Chuckwalla address and came up with a house on a country road in the middle of the desert. There was very little around it that made up a town.

He looked at Ivy and Cooper, who were now ignoring him and were locked in a passionate embrace. Apparently, their anger and distrust had blown over as quickly as it flared up. He knew they were both forgiving people—otherwise he'd never have been accepted into their good graces after what he'd done. The sight relaxed him... and made him horny.

"Okay, you guys. Either we're all going back to bed or to Arizona. Can you kiss and make up later?" He scooped up Blair's junk and crammed it all back into her stinky purse. He had something, at least, that he could give to her mom now.

Ivy pulled away with a small giggle. "Let's go."

"I have an address in Chuckwalla finally," Bodhi added as they trooped back out to Cooper's car. "Just no phone number."

Cooper adjusted himself with a grin and winked at Bodhi. "Oh, I forgot to tell you, I was able to get the presidential suite for tonight at the nicest hotel near Yuma. It's a brand-new resort called the Western Regency Palace."

"Sounds interesting—I guess," Bodhi said with a shrug. He was anxious to get going.

Finally, they were on the road. They headed east on Interstate 8 through the California desert of eastern San Diego County. The scenery was completely different from Del Mar. While Del Mar was graced with beautiful homes, hills, and the ocean, this area consisted of mile after mile of uncultivated scrub brush. Bodhi commented that the place was "as hot and dry as a popcorn fart."

The rocky terrain flattened out considerably as they entered Imperial County and passed by El Centro where there was a fair amount of agriculture. But that gave way to a flat, desolate desert as they got closer to Yuma.

Since the scenery didn't provide them with much in the way of entertainment, they decided to amuse themselves by talking about their families and the foibles of their most colorful relatives.

Bodhi told them, "My great-aunt Mildred used to store her potholders in the oven, and then she'd forget and turn it on. They caught fire several times, resulting in a lot of black smoke billowing out of her door. The fire department tried talking to her, but her solution was to disconnect the fire alarm instead of listening to them. The landlord finally booted her out because he was sure she'd burn down the building. She went into assisted living after that and lived there until she passed away at ninety-four."

Cooper went next. "Most of my family has been pretty normal, but I have a cousin who's tried to hire our family law firm several times. He likes to pretend he's been hurt someplace like a market or restaurant and has filed close to fifty unjustifiable nuisance claims. He's a real piece of work." Cooper laughed. "He actually wanted to be a lawyer himself at one point until he discovered he needed to study to do it. He flunked out of law school after his first semester. He's the epitome of someone with his hand out for an easy score." He looked in the rear-view mirror at Ivy and asked, "Any colorful folks in your family tree, babe?"

She guffawed in an unladylike manner and said, "Remember, I grew up in Chicago, so any distant ties I might have to the mafia may or may not be greatly exaggerated." Then she added with a laugh, "My mom's mom had an interesting Christmas tradition, though."

"Yeah?" asked Bodhi. "What was that?"

Ivy looked out the window and chuckled. "My grandparents liked to travel, but my grandmother was a little disorganized. She tended to forget to leave her hotel or motel key at the desk when they checked out. Back then they were real keys that hung from big plastic fobs. The fobs had the hotel address on them, and you were supposed to drop the key in a mailbox if you forgot to return it. The hotels must have hated having to make keys all the time. Anyway, one year my grandmother took all of the keys she hadn't returned and hung them on the Christmas tree. She said they were all 'good memories' and were better than fancy glass balls."

As the miles sped by and they got closer and closer to their destination, the purpose of their trip settled over them and they stopped trying to entertain each other. It was not going to be the least bit enjoyable to face Blair's mother with their news.

"Bodhi?" Ivy asked softly.

"Hmm?"

"What are you going to tell her about Blair?"

Bodhi sighed. "I'm not sure. I'll be as honest as I can without being hurtful, and I guess I'll just wing it. Maybe she knows more than we think she knows. It's impossible to tell until we get there." He turned to look at his friends. "But thank you both for coming with me. It means a lot."

Chapter Twenty-Three

When they arrived at their hotel, the front desk clerk made certain to point out that the sofa in the sitting room folded out into the other bed they would need. All three of them smiled benignly at that bit of information. As it turned out, the presidential suite was a gaudy room with laughable décor. The throw pillows were all in the shapes of cacti—minus the prickly stickers—and the paintings on the wall depicted desert scenes of dubious interest including rattlesnakes and sun-bleached animal skulls. The southwestern "earth tones" were over the top with vivid oranges, browns, purples, and turquoise that hurt their eyes. At least the bed looked comfortable, the room was clean, and they had a nice view of the desert and the Gila Mountains.

Once they dumped their bags and freshened up, they headed to the restaurant off the hotel lobby. Aiming to partake in the local cuisine, Bodhi ordered a Sonoran hotdog that turned out to be wrapped in bacon and grilled, served on a bolillo-style hot dog bun, and topped with pinto beans. On the side he had raw onions, tomatoes, mayo, mustard, and a hot jalapeno salsa that he avoided like the plague.

Cooper decided to try Quechan stew, hoping for an authentic Native American dish. When it arrived, he discovered it was an unimaginative bowl of chili that would have been too spicy for Bodhi. But it did come with an interesting fry bread on the side. And not one to miss out on the local color and flavor, Ivy ordered Navajo chicken tacos. The tacos were also made with the delicious fry bread, and they all decided she'd ordered the best dish.

"Winner, winner, chicken dinner!" she chanted and then bit into a yummy taco, laughing at their jealous expressions. "Or... lunch anyway," she said with a smile.

All too soon, lunch was over and it was time to track down Lauren Henry. They headed to the car they'd left in the underground lot and programmed the GPS for 635 Saguaro Road, Chuckwalla.

"I hope she's there," muttered Bodhi. "A lot of Arizona residents head to the coast when it's this hot." Knowing that already, no one answered him. It was common knowledge in San Diego County that Arizonans invaded their area during the summer months.

They headed north out of Yuma, and the scenery grew more and more desolate. Finally, after navigating off the main highway, they came to a small town that proclaimed itself to be "Chuckwalla, founded in 1899, population 4016." As they get closer to the town center, they drove by the Rep-Tile Flooring Company, the Lizard Lounge, and the Chuckwalla All-You-Can-Eat Buffet. Their GPS directed them to go east just past the restaurant, and that put them smack-dab onto Saguaro Road. When he saw the street sign, Bodhi's stomach did a queasy flip, and he was immediately sorry about having the Sonoran hotdog. He popped a mint into his mouth and watched how the heat waves shimmered off the pavement in front of them. The thermometer on Cooper's dashboard said it was 111º.

"How do people live in heat like this?" asked Ivy.

"I dunno," answered Cooper. "But they seem to manage just fine up in Las Vegas. It's sure not my style. Give me the beach any day and forget the desert." He looked to the right at a medium-sized house that more or less matched all of the other houses around it in style. "Here we are."

He pulled up to the curbless front of the property and carefully parked where he wasn't blocking the driveway or mailbox. The yard was neat and filled with small rocks where he would have expected a grassy lawn. "I guess watering the grass is out of the question around here," he observed. "Those plants all must be drought-resistant." He eyed the scrubby little plants that sprouted up here and there amongst the stones. It was a terribly drab sight. The only color came from some painted pots on either side of the front door. There was no shade anywhere.

"Here goes nothing," announced Bodhi. He took a deep breath and stepped out of the car, closely followed by Ivy and Cooper. They all squinted in the bright sunlight, even with their sunglasses on, and gasped at the blast of the hot, dry air. "It feels like a furnace out here," he complained. "I can appreciate the underground parking at the hotel now. This is unbelievable."

They all headed to the door. Bodhi carried a shopping bag with Blair's purse and other junk in it. He rang the bell and heard a woman's voice calling, "Coming!" cheerfully from inside.

A middle-aged woman flung open the door with an eager smile on her face, but her happiness disappeared and her expression turned guarded when she noticed all of their solemn faces. Her large blue eyes were eerily identical to Blair's, and she was also tall and blonde. Puffy shadows under her eyes and deep frown lines kept her from being pretty, but she may have been once. Time had not been kind to this lady.

"Lauren Henry?" Bodhi asked.

"Yes. And you would be...?" Her raspy voice suggested years of cigarette smoking.

"I'm Bodhi Monaghan, and these are my fr—"

He didn't have a chance to finish his introductions because Lauren flung her arms around Bodhi's neck and cried happily,

"Bodhi, darling!" Bodhi cringed as she kissed his cheek. "Come in, come in, son!" She appeared confused as she stepped back to let them in. "Who are these lovely people and where is my beautiful Blair? Why isn't she with you all? I'm so glad to meet you! You're *so* handsome, Bodhi! No wonder Blair fell for you. I've heard so much about your fancy wedding in London! That naughty daughter of mine promised photos and never sent any. I wanted to be there for it so badly, but I just didn't have the money for the trip, especially after I was burglarized." She prattled on and on with a machine-gun speed of delivery, barely pausing to take a breath. All Bodhi could think was that he was happy the house was air-conditioned, but this was worse than he'd feared.

Bodhi tried again. "Mrs. Henry—"

"Oh, silly! Call me Mom, darling!" Lauren interrupted, squeezing his arm.

"No thank you, ma'am. I think it's best if we all sit down, Mrs. Henry." Despite the ice-cold air, Bodhi felt a trickle of sweat dribble down his back. After she sat and they all found places in her crowded living room, he began again. "These are my friends Ivy Chambers and Cooper Houston. They were also fr... acquaintances of Blair's. We all live together."

"Where is she, son?"

"Please, ma'am, don't call me that. I'm sorry to have to tell you that your daughter passed away recently."

Lauren gasped. Her eyes filled and she shook her head in denial.

Bodhi forced himself to keep going. "I didn't know your whereabouts until just a couple of days ago and had no way to contact you. It wasn't even until this morning that we found your actual address. I'm so sorry about your daughter."

After some dramatic chest grabbing, face-pulling, and lots of blinking until she produced some tears that trickled down her cheeks, Lauren choked out, "Was it the cancer? Did it take her?"

Bodhi's eyes narrowed. This was Blair's mother; he knew she had to be devastated by his news, but her reaction felt forced and dishonest. He didn't get it. He'd just told her that her daughter had died, and what he saw looked like bad acting.

Lauren continued in the hushed tone one often hears at a funeral, "I thought she said the doctor in London had cured her, and she was so excited to be getting married now that she was healthy. You must be devastated. Is that why you didn't get married? But wait... Blair said you *did* get married, so...?" She furrowed her brows at Bodhi.

Ivy spotted a box of tissues nearby and set them down in front of Lauren before taking her seat again silently.

Bodhi looked at Ivy and Cooper as if to judge just how truthful to be, and they gave him understanding smiles. So, he went on, "Blair was not cured of her cancer, and she and I never married—no matter what she told you. It wasn't because she was sick. It was because I didn't love her or even know her very well. I quit my job in London and left—not knowing she was even ill. I never had plans to see her again, but she found me and followed me back to where I live in California. Apparently, she thought she could use me to buy her medical insurance."

"I don't understand. Why would she lie to me?" Her blue eyes grew even larger.

"I don't know, ma'am. Maybe to spare you from worrying?"

"Well, it was nice of you to pay her way to see that doctor in London. I know she wanted to be part of his study." Her voice cracked. "I have to thank you for giving her the money to get there."

Bodhi looked down at his feet and rubbed his forehead. This was clearly not going well. "Why," he began, looking at her finally, "did you think I paid her way to London?"

"She told me so!"

"I didn't meet Blair until she was already in London, and even then, I barely knew her. She wormed her way into my life and pretended to everyone that we were going to get married. I have good reason to believe she drugged me to get into my apartment and my bed, and then later she drugged me a second time to get her way."

Anger took the place of the sadness on Lauren's face as she spluttered, "That's a horrible accusation, young man! My Blair was a beautiful, talented young woman who was dealt a bad lot in life and came down with a terrible disease. And you're bad-mouthing her? How dare you!"

Bodhi looked like he was getting ready to say something awful, so Cooper took that moment to derail her outburst and asked, "Mrs. Henry, didn't you say you'd been burglarized? Were you possibly missing some jewelry?"

Her head snapped toward Cooper, and she answered, "Yes. A couple of years ago, I inherited my mother's entire collection of estate jewels. She was from a very well-to-do family, you know. And here I thought she'd disowned me." She gave a weak smile and dabbed at her eyes. "It was such a surprise to hear from her lawyer. But what does that have to do with anything? And what happened to my darling Blair?"

"Could you describe some of the jewelry, please?" asked Cooper in a soft, polite voice.

Frowning slightly, Lauren said, "Mother had some lovely pieces. Some antique jet earrings... Well, and other earrings too, but I just loved those. Several cocktail rings—my favorite was a large opal surrounded by diamonds. It was quite valuable, you know. There was a Cartier watch, a topaz and garnet brooch, and a wonderful necklace and bracelet set that was twenty-two karat gold and had a gorgeous pendant of a bird that was encrusted with rubies, sapphires, diamonds, and emeralds. It was breathtaking, and it killed me to have it stolen. I could never afford any insurance for it all."

Bodhi nodded knowingly and explained, "I have some good news and some bad news for you. First of all, you weren't burglarized at all, and I have some of your jewelry for you." Lauren's eyes widened at him. "But the bad news is that it was Blair who stole from you—probably to fund her own trip to the study in London. I don't have everything you mentioned, so some of it must have been pawned or sold." He reached into the shopping bag and produced a baggie filled with the pieces he'd found in Blair's purse.

"Oh! My birdie!" cried Lauren as she snatched the bag to her bosom. She sounded like a child. Bodhi cringed inwardly and looked away. He was beginning to see how Blair could have been a little messed up. This woman didn't exactly seem like she had both oars in the water.

She admired her loot for a moment as the others watched her silently. Then she looked up and asked, "You said Blair followed you to California. Does that mean she died there?"

"Yes, ma'am," Bodhi answered. "From what I can gather, the doctor in London couldn't help her. He referred her to a special clinic in California, knowing they were conducting their own trial. I'm sorry to say she was turned down because her cancer was too advanced."

"Oh." Lauren dropped her bag of goodies into her lap and grabbed a tissue. She dabbed her eyes. "Well, at least I got my stuff back—or some of it anyway." She made a sour face. "Blair was always a problem child, you know. I guess I'm not surprised she's been lying and stealing."

Bodhi thought he had whiplash. Just a moment before Blair was beautiful and talented, and now she was a lying, stealing bother? "You have no idea," he muttered under his breath. He took that moment to look around the room and noticed several table surfaces and the fireplace mantle had photos of Blair. She seemed to have been in a few local pageants, judging from the outfits and sashes. The pageants must have started when she was about five years old. A large, framed picture in the middle of the mantle showed Blair wearing a tiara and a sash proclaiming her to be Chuckwalla Tumbleweed Festival Princess. The cheesy smile and vacant look in Blair's eyes creeped Bodhi out.

Deciding he'd had enough, Bodhi placed the shopping bag in front of Lauren and said, "There are a few more of Blair's things in this. I'm sorry we got rid of the rest of her clothes. She didn't have a lot, really, but you ought to have these."

Lauren pawed through the contents of the bag murmuring, "What a lovely fragrance." She breathed it in as if savoring it, making the others cringe to themselves. Then she pulled out the passport. "Hendrix?" she asked. "Who's Hendrix?"

"That's how Blair introduced herself to me, so I believed it was her name. Then the doctor at the clinic said it was Henry. Do you think the passport is a fake possibly?"

"I don't know. It could be. I didn't have a birth certificate for her because she was... um... well... Let's just say I was too young to be having a daughter. I'm sure you can tell by looking at me that we were often mistaken for sisters," she simpered as the others tried to keep a straight face. "Anyway, she was very upset about the birth certificate problem. We fought about it, actually. Eventually she said she'd get a passport somehow, and I shouldn't worry about it." She paused a moment. "That was right before the burglary..." Lauren sighed and then asked suddenly, "Was she in a lot of pain?"

This was the moment Bodhi had feared the most. "I don't think she suffered too badly," he explained evasively. "She was very tired and slept a lot... toward the end." He dreaded telling Lauren that her daughter had taken her own life. And no way in the world did he want to bring up the false pregnancy claims.

But Lauren surprised them all by snapping at Bodhi. "Tell me the truth, young man. I know my daughter was not one who *enjoyed* suffering, and she told me before she left for England that if she couldn't get treatment she'd kill herself. So, how'd she do it? Pills?"

"Oh, uh, no. Actually, she jumped off the Coronado Bridge."

Lauren's eyes lit up and she smiled victoriously. "That's my girl! She went out in style her own way! Did they find her body?"

"Yes. They did right away. And I took care of her... remains. She was cremated and the Telophase Society did an off-shore burial at sea. I hope that's all right with you."

"It's fine. She always liked water. Maybe that's why the bridge appealed to her. When she was little, she asked all the time to go see the ocean." Lauren held up the baggie of loot again and smiled at it.

Bodhi's stomach roiled, and he felt the beginning of a migraine stabbing at him. It was time to get out of here. He stood and nodded at Ivy and Cooper. "Mrs. Henry, I'm terribly sorry for your loss, and I'm sorry we had so much bad news for you, but I think we ought to be on our way now. We have a long drive ahead of us."

Ivy blinked at him, and Cooper stood, giving him a small, understanding smile. They both shook hands with Lauren and offered her their condolences, then scooted toward the door. They watched as Lauren draped herself around Bodhi in a far too friendly manner, whispering something into his ear.

Bodhi winced and extracted himself quickly as he stepped out of her clutches. "Ma'am," was all he said with a curt nod and then bolted for the door. "Let's get the fuck out of here," he muttered to his friends as they rushed out.

"What did she say to you, Bodhi?" Ivy asked with a small smirk. "You sure wanted to get out of there in a hurry."

"She told me to ditch the two losers and come back to party with her tonight. Apparently, she's quite proud of her skills involving dicks and her mouth. She also has a platinum pussy I shouldn't miss. Something tells me that's how she makes her living because she didn't offer it for free."

Ivy made a gagging sound.

"If it's okay with the two of you, I'd really rather just get our shit and get out of this place. I'll be happy to drive back if you're tired, Coop."

Cooper smiled at his friend and said, "I'm fine. Let's go grab our stuff and head home. I've seen enough of Chuckwalla. I need to breathe some ocean air before I choke."

As they walked back to the car, Ivy noticed that Bodhi was limping more than usual. *That scrape on his leg must be bothering him*, she thought. But just then a wasp buzzed around her head, and she frantically swatted it away, forgetting about Bodhi's limp.

When they were in the roasting car again, Cooper cranked up the AC as high as it would go and hit the gas.

Chapter Twenty-Four

As they drove back toward Yuma, Bodhi's headache grew worse and worse, and he was sweating through his shirt. As he rubbed his forehead and tried to loosen the muscles in his neck, Cooper looked over at him. "You okay? You're looking kind of pale all of a sudden."

At that moment, Bodhi's sweating stopped, and he started shivering. He growled, "I'll be fine if you turn down the AC."

"Sure thing. It was just so hot when we got in…" Cooper looked back at the road and turned the air down to a normal temperature. Then he noticed out of the corner of his eye that Bodhi was kneading the muscle of his thigh just above his knee. "Is your leg bothering you?"

"Yeah. It aches like a motherfucker."

"I have some ibuprofen in my purse. Would you like some?" Ivy asked. "Here's some water too. It's probably pretty warm by now from sitting in the car, but it ought to help." She passed two pills and the water bottle to the front seat for Bodhi, who accepted them gratefully. "Has it been hurting all day?"

"A little. It's a lot worse all of a sudden, though." He swallowed the pills down with a chug of water and fumbled as he tried to recap the bottle. "I think I need to close my eyes for a wh…" he mumbled. The plastic bottle hit the floor where it rolled under the seat, spilling water all over the carpet. Instead of his head leaning back, he pitched sideways and clonked his head on the window. Then he pitched forward, and it looked like lights out.

"Bodhi?" Cooper looked back at his buddy again with a startled expression. "Hey, man, are you okay?"

"What's wrong, Cooper?" Ivy asked. "Bodhi? *Bodhi?* Cooper, did he just faint? What's going on with him?"

"Naturally, we're out in the sticks," Cooper growled. "Ivy, I'm going to keep heading to Yuma, but I think you need to call 911. He's completely out of it, and he's shaking like a leaf."

"Oh, Bodhi," she whimpered plaintively. "Okay, I'm calling right now." She paused while the dispatcher connected the call and asked the nature of her emergency. "Oh, um, hi. We're in a car heading south to Yuma on State Road 95. My friend just passed out and he's shaking... No, I wouldn't call it a seizure, but what do I know? It's more like he's shivering, but he looks really bad! No, he definitely hasn't taken any drugs except ibuprofen just a minute ago. We need to get him to a hospital... Yes, okay. We're just about ten or fifteen minutes south of Chuckwalla. We're in a Silver Range Rover with California plates." She gave the license number. "Okay, we'll keep driving closer to Yuma." Ivy paused to listen. "Cooper, she says the highway patrol is going to lead us there and an ambulance is on its way from Yuma to meet us. She says to keep driving, and I'm supposed to stay on the line until they get to us."

A few minutes later, they could hear sirens coming at them from behind, so Cooper turned on his flashing emergency lights. Soon a trooper passed them and said over a loudspeaker to follow right behind him.

"Okay, the patrolman is leading us now. Thank you for your help! What should I do for him until we see the ambulance? No! I'm not driving; I'm a passenger. Okay, I can do that. Thanks for your help." She hung up the phone and looked frantically at Cooper, who was white-knuckle driving as fast as the patrol car ahead of him would allow with the siren blaring the entire time. "She just said to make sure he's not choking on anything."

Bodhi was still out cold, and his face was a pasty gray. This went on for another ten minutes or so, until finally they heard the welcome sound of another siren coming from the opposite direction. Ivy was beside herself with worry when the patrol car signaled that he was pulling over onto the shoulder of the highway. Cooper followed suit.

Within moments after the ambulance made an emergency U-turn—in thankfully light traffic—the EMT guys had Bodhi on a stretcher, hooked to IV fluids, and were loading him into their vehicle. He looked dreadful and hadn't regained consciousness, even when they dragged him out of the car and stuck an IV in his arm. The EMTs said that his heart rate was accelerated and his breathing shallow.

Cooper and Ivy clung to each other as they watched the proceedings. Both had eyes as round as saucers. They tried their best to answer the questions from the emergency crew, giving them Bodhi's name, age, and what they knew about his leg hurting. They also verified that he had complained about a bad headache before passing out. Neither knew of any underlying health conditions other than some extreme stress of late. Bodhi had never mentioned any autoimmune or genetic issues, and they knew he wasn't diabetic.

As they spoke with one of the EMTs, the other one cut off Bodhi's pant leg, revealing a highly inflamed wound. Red streaks were running up and down his leg. It looked horribly infected.

In a hushed whisper, Ivy spoke to Cooper, "Ohmygod! How was he managing with that leg in such a mess? He must have been in agony. Why didn't he say anything? Did you see this?"

"I haven't paid any attention to it since we got him patched up right after it happened. We were kind of... um... preoccupied after that. But now I'm sure sorry," Cooper murmured back to her. "I thought we should have taken him to the ER when it happened, but he kept saying it was fine. Obviously, he needed stitches and something stronger than over-the-counter anti-biotic ointment. Damn it, Bodhi." He looked up as one of the paramedics addressed them.

"Sir, you can meet us at the hospital in Yuma. We'll get him there quickly, but I can't recommend that you try following us while our siren's going." The EMT gave Cooper the name and address of the hospital so he could program it into his GPS, and they took off in a blaze of flashing lights and noise.

Ivy started to cry. "I feel so awful for Bodhi. He's been trying so hard to do the right thing for everyone, and he just keeps having shit thrown at him."

"Yeah, I agree," Cooper said in a grim voice. "Let's get going. I'm sure he's going to need us when he comes to." He didn't want to think of the possibility of Bodhi *not* coming to. He realized he'd always thought of Bodhi as a continual presence in his life, and losing him was inconceivable. Having him out of the country had been painful enough...

The state trooper cautioned Cooper, "Drive sensibly and get yourselves there safely, sir. I hope your friend is okay."

They thanked him for the escort and took off at the speed limit. He followed them for a while and then took an exit, flashing his lights at them. Cooper waved.

Ivy asked suddenly, "Should we call his parents? Do you have a contact for them in Hawaii?"

"I think we should call them, but I'd have to get the number from Bodhi's phone. It's probably still in his pocket. I'm guess-ing he has it written down somewhere around the house, too, but a lot of good that'll do us."

"Do you know what town they live in? If it's not someplace big like Honolulu, maybe we can track them down."

Cooper racked his brain to remember. "I know it's on Maui. And it's not Lahaina." He shook his head. "Hana? That doesn't sound right either. See if you can pull up a map on your phone and read off some of the names to me. Maybe one will sound right."

So, as Cooper tried to drive and think, Ivy read off town after town to him.

"They all sound alike," he complained after the tenth or so try. Then he remembered, "There's a bay there. Oh, and his parents like to play golf. Look for golf courses."

"Okay. King Kamehameha, Wailea, Kaanapali, Kaanapali Kai, Kapalua…"

"That's it! Kapalua Bay! I remember Bodhi mentioning that. Maybe you can find a listing for them, or you can call a realtor or something, and someone will recognize the name."

"It's a pretty populated area, but I'll see if I can do a people search first. What are his parents' names? Oh wait! I remember him saying his mom's name is Peach. That's not common at all. We ought to be able to find a Peach Monaghan."

Ivy did a bunch of searches through public records, and lo and behold, there was a Peach married to Emmett Monaghan who lived in the Kapalua area. "I found them," she cried happily. "Now what do I tell them, Cooper?" She could tell by the scenery and the GPS that they were almost at the hospital at this point.

"See if you can get hold of them first and tell them what we know so far—which isn't much."

So, Ivy dialed the number she'd found and was immediately connected to a soft-spoken lady. "Mrs. Monaghan? This is Ivy Chambers, Bodhi's… uh… friend. We're in Arizona and Bodhi has been taken to the hospital. We thought you ought to know." She went on to explain to Bodhi's horrified mother everything she knew about Bodhi's injury and passing out. "Maybe it was just from the heat, but I have to say, it didn't look too good. Cooper and I thought we should call you, and maybe the doctors can tell you more. We're just entering the hospital now." There was a pause, and then Ivy answered, "Yes, as soon as we can. We'll let you know. I'm sorry to call with news like this." Another pause. "Alright. You have my number now and you can call me anytime. We'll speak soon." She disconnected and looked at Cooper. "I hope that was a smart move. She sounded terrible and was cursing the fact that they moved away from their one and only son, even if he was living in England for part of the time. Now the poor woman is scared to death."

"So am I," Cooper replied.

Chapter Twenty-Five

After hounding everyone in the ER, they finally found someone who could tell them that Bodhi had been taken to surgery and that the surgeons were working to save his leg.

Ivy began to cry again, and Cooper felt like he might hurl. The idea of Bodhi with a leg missing? *He'd hate living that way!* Cooper thought to himself. *Surely with medicine as advanced as it is now, someone doesn't lose their leg from a simple scratch—well, a big, deep scratch that needed stitches no doubt.*

Then he thought of the number of times the beaches had been closed over the years due to polluted water, and things started looking a lot grimmer. He knew that swimming in the Children's Pool in La Jolla was almost always prohibited due to bacteria levels from the harbor seals who'd taken up residence there. They had basically turned the small cove that was protected by an old seawall into a disgusting seal toilet. Windansea wasn't usually a problem though. *I guess it just takes one bad microbe in the wrong place,* he groaned to himself.

Ivy made another call to Maui to update Bodhi's parents and reported back to Cooper, "They're getting on the next plane out. I guess it's a night flight, and they'll be here in the morning."

"They're really nice people. I'm sorry you never met them before, but you'll like them," Cooper assured her. "I'm glad they're coming. Bodhi's never said much, but I think he's missed them."

They sat for what felt like hours—even though it wasn't actually—waiting and waiting for some news, when a nurse came into the waiting room asking for Cooper Houston. He sprang up like a jack-in-the-box when he heard her call his name. She indicated that they should follow her to the nurses' station.

"Mr. Monaghan's medical records list you as his emergency contact, so I'm glad you're here. He's being moved upstairs to a room now, and you'll be able to see him. He's had his wound cleaned and fixed up by the surgeon, but there is still a great danger of further infection because whatever hit him…"

"It was a surfboard," interrupted Cooper.

"Yes, well, it actually cracked his tibia, and the worry is that the bone will become infected. If that happens, it's gravely serious."

Ivy grabbed Cooper's hand and tried to keep herself from crying again.

Dragging his other hand through his hair, Cooper asked in a shaky voice, "So, what's happening with him now?" He felt some measure of relief to hear that Bodhi still had both legs—for now at least.

"He's getting massive amounts of antibiotics as well as pain meds. He's pretty out of it, but you can certainly talk to him. Just don't expect much of a response, and please don't say anything that will upset him." She gave Cooper a serious, no-joke look. "Does he have family nearby?" she asked.

Speaking up finally, Ivy announced, "*We're* his family. We all live together—in Del Mar, California. But his parents are flying in from Hawaii and will be here in the morning."

The nurse eyed them and looked like she was about to ask how they were all family, and thought better of it. "He's on the sixth floor," she said. "Room 606. Good luck. I hope he gets better quickly." She gave them a weak smile, pointed them toward the elevators, and left.

Cooper wound his arm around Ivy's shoulders as they made their way down the long corridor. Neither knew what to say until they were inside the elevator. "I feel so guilty," Ivy moaned. "Why didn't we insist that he needed to get that thing looked at right away?"

"Bodhi wouldn't have listened. You know that. He wanted to get home and forget about the shitty day he'd had, and he wanted to play as much as you and I did." He kissed the top of her head. "Don't beat yourself up about it, honey. But... just so you know... I feel horribly guilty too." The elevator dinged and they were let out into another shiny hallway where they looked for a sign that would direct them to room 606.

Once they arrived on Bodhi's floor, they had to sign in at the nurses' station. After not getting any pertinent information from anyone, they both steeled themselves, trying to find a way to look positive for Bodhi.

It turned out he'd been admitted to a glass-walled room in the intensive care unit. The vision that greeted them as they entered his open door deflated every bit of upbeat thinking they could muster.

Bodhi lay hooked up to an IV and several monitors that seemed to be measuring all of his vitals. An oxygen canula was attached to his nose, and his face looked gray. Worst of all, he still seemed to be shaking.

"Bodhi?" Ivy asked softly. "Are you awake?" She reached out to stroke his hand.

No response.

"Hey man, we're here for you," Cooper announced unnecessarily. He turned to Ivy and said, "Oh, for crying out loud. There's something about facing this kind of situation that makes me dumb. Put me in a courtroom and I'm the great orator. Stick me in front of a beloved friend who's suffering, and I turn into a bumbling idiot." He tried to laugh at himself, but it turned into a groan. Then he dragged a couple of chairs up to the bed. Looking at Ivy, he saw fresh tears streaking down her face. "Come on, babe. None of that," he whispered, wiping her cheek. "We're supposed to cheer him up."

"Cooper, I'm afraid I've been mean to Bodhi. I hate myself!"

"What are you talking about? How have you been mean to him? I haven't seen anything like that from you."

A fresh sob bubbled up, and Ivy covered her face with her hands. When she composed herself, she answered, "I should have been honest and told him that I still love him instead of stringing him along. It's like I've been punishing him."

"Is it true? Are you back to loving *him*?" Cooper's face turned red, and he looked at her with narrowed eyes.

"Of course I love him," she whisper-shouted. "In some ways, I never stopped."

Cooper's face twisted in agony. "Where does that leave me in this scenario?"

Ivy's jaw dropped. "Cooper! Give me some credit. Do you think I'd be *that* fickle?"

"I don't know anything anymore, Ivy. My best buddy is lying here fighting for his life, and you're being cryptic." His voice rose in volume, despite his attempt to control it. "My brain isn't exactly *processing* things really well at the moment, and everything is a mess!"

Just then, an alarm went off on Bodhi's vast array of connected equipment, and he started to shake harder and moan.

"Oh, shit. Ivy, we need to shut up. They said not to upset him, and here we go doing just that."

As Cooper spoke, a stern-faced nurse rushed into the room. She'd heard his last statement, so she asked them, "Would the two of you take it outside? Mr. Monaghan needs his rest!" She shut off the alarm, checked Bodhi's IV, and adjusted a couple of things while they stood staring at her. Turning to them she said, "Well?"

Chastised, Cooper said humbly, "We promise we'll behave. Please don't kick us out. We both love him, and we're sorry for acting like dopes."

She narrowed her eyes at him and answered, "One more argument in front of him, and you're outta here for good. Got it?"

"We get it," Ivy said in a soft, pleading voice. "We'll be careful." She looked at Cooper and said, "*Never* doubt my love for you."

That seemed to soften up the nurse a bit, but she gave them a sour look before she left.

Sighing, Cooper relaxed. "I'm sorry. I know you love me. And I agree you need to tell Bodhi as soon as possible that you love him too. I'm still not sure what this means for us getting married but somehow, we need to work it out so that he's happy too... if that's what you want. I can't see him hurt again."

Ivy thought a moment and then said, "When Bodhi gets better, I think all three of us ought to have a chat with my friend Casey. He's in a triad and he's probably the happiest man I've ever known. They even have the cutest little girl. He's shown me about a million photos of her." She continued to softly stroke Bodhi's hand while she spoke. "Maybe we could meet all three of them and get some pointers."

"That sounds like a good idea." Cooper nodded, and his stomach growled. "You hungry?" he asked. "I'm starved, and it doesn't look like our boy here is going to sit up and start demanding to get out of here very soon. I could go get us some dinner and bring it back, if you want to stay with him and keep him company for a while."

"Um... I guess." She shrugged. "I'm not really hungry."

"Do you need anything from the hotel?"

"I don't think so, but I guess it's good we didn't give up the room. Do you think we ought to reserve a few more nights?"

"Good thinking. I think I'll run back and talk to them, take a quick shower, and I'll bring back some burgers or something. I'll be quick, but I've never sweat so much in my life, and I desperately need a clean shirt." He gave her a kiss and then leaned over to kiss Bodhi on the forehead. "Hang in there, man. I'll see you soon," he choked out. Seeming to think better of his plan, he looked at Ivy. "Do you want to come with me?"

"I'd rather stay here so he's not alone."

Nodding, Cooper said, "That's what I thought. Okay, I'll be back as soon as I can." Walking away, he thought it was selfish of him to feel hungry, but he knew he couldn't help what his body needed. "What a clusterfuck," he mumbled as he headed out to his car.

Chapter Twenty-Six

Cooper's quick shower and a fresh change of clothes made him feel nearly human again. He booked the room for three more nights, which seemed to thrill the front desk manager. Idly, he wondered how much business they actually had. Heading out to a nearby hamburger restaurant, he called his dad from his car to explain that he would need a few days off from work. He'd already told his father most of Bodhi's story, but the parts about the surfing injury and the trip to Arizona were new information.

"Give Bodhi my best, Cooper. I hope all goes well for him. You're a good friend to stick with him like this through the difficult times. Your mother will be happy to know we raised you to have your heart in the right place."

"Thanks, Dad." Cooper felt himself getting choked up. His father wasn't usually sentimental. "I'm so scared for him," he whispered.

"He's young and fit and strong. He'll pull through, son. We'll keep him in our prayers in any case, though. Don't forget to take care of yourself too. And don't worry about your clients. Your sister and I will make sure everyone's happy."

Cooper promised to keep his family in the loop and pulled in to order some dinner.

* * *

When he got back to the hospital, he rushed up to the sixth floor, nervous to find out if anything had changed for the better… or…no, he wouldn't think about the worse. He found Ivy snuggled up as close to Bodhi as her chair would allow. Her head was resting on his shoulder, and she had his unencumbered arm in her hands. It looked to Cooper as though she'd been crying again, but was exhausted from all of the emotion. He hated to disturb her, but he also thought having something in her stomach would help. The tacos she'd eaten had been hours and hours ago by now as it was after ten o'clock.

"Ivy? I have a burger for you and your favorite milkshake. Do you want to have some food?" Cooper had always looked for practical, tangible ways of helping.

She opened her eyes, smiled up at him, and answered, "Bodhi woke up for a moment."

"Did he say anything?"

Ivy scoffed. "He said, and I quote, 'I feel like shit.' Then he groaned and went back to sleep. At least it was something. Unfortunately, he still has a high fever according to the nurse, so they took him out for an x-ray or scan or something. No one said anything when they brought him back, so I guess they don't know anything yet. Typical. I hate waiting for news." She took a whiff of the air and said, "I'll take that burger now, please. Where's yours?"

"I was so starved, I scarfed it down while I drove over here."

"My guess is I shouldn't eat it in here. I'll just pop down to the lounge at the end of the hall. Want to come with me?"

"Visiting hours end in less than an hour, babe. I'm not about to leave him alone any longer than we have to. Is that okay?" He sat down and handed her a bag and a drink.

"I understand, and I'll just be a minute." She took off with her food and fairly wolfed it down so she could get right back, but she also had an important call to make.

As soon as Ivy returned, she mentioned, "I phoned my assistant, and she assured me she'll have things under control. She said her mom could come in and help with sales too. Apparently, she's been itching to do something useful and has hinted that she'd love to work in the gallery part-time." Ivy gave a tired smile. "It's a huge relief."

Cooper had arranged himself close to Bodhi. He needed contact so badly until he got some reassurance that Bodhi was going to be fine. Ivy mirrored Cooper's position on Bodhi's other side.

At 10:45, a young doctor came in, gave them a grim smile, and took a look at Bodhi's leg. He checked the computer screen that had all of Bodhi's vital signs on it and wordlessly made some entries into the file.

"How's he doing?" Cooper finally asked. He didn't like the silent treatment or the suspense.

"I'm sorry to say, the infection has invaded the tibia. We'll monitor his condition throughout the night, but we may have to make a serious call in the next few hours. He's not responding as well to the antibiotics as I'd have hoped, frankly."

"Doesn't he have to sign something for you to...?" Cooper looked pointedly at Bodhi's infected leg and shuddered. He couldn't voice his thought.

"We will do everything to save his life, and if it comes to needing further, more extreme surgery, we'll do our best to get Mr. Monaghan's permission."

Cooper sat up straighter and announced, "I'm his lawyer, and his best friend. Also, his emergency contact."

"Yes, well, that's good to know, but it still doesn't give you permission to make decisions for him. That is, unless he has an Advance Directive that gives the decision-making power to you. Does he?"

"Not to my knowledge."

"It's understandable." The doctor gave a small sigh. "Men his age don't usually think of things like that until they have a family. You may want to discuss it with him sometime. In any case, I'm going to add another antibiotic to his medications and see if we have more luck with the combination. Amputation is always a terribly difficult call to make, but our first and foremost goal is always to save the patient's life."

Cooper looked at Ivy who once again had tears in her eyes, a quivering lip, and a face as pale as the sheets on Bodhi's bed. He addressed the doctor shakily, "His parents will be here in a few hours. They're flying in from Hawaii. Surely you can wait on such a serious surgery until they get here."

"All I can say is, we'll see. If his fever doesn't decrease soon, we worry about brain damage... and worse. The most important thing right now is to keep him from going into septic shock."

Cooper quickly regretted the food he'd just eaten.

Looking at Bodhi's face, he saw his buddy's eyes squeeze together. Then Bodhi's mouth moved.

"Did you just say something, Bodhi? Look, I think he's coming around a little."

The doctor leaned over and spoke clearly, "Mr. Monaghan, can you hear me?"

With a protracted moan, Bodhi croaked, "Don't you dare." Then his face went slack, and he seemed to be sleeping once more.

Raising his eyebrows, Cooper pointed out, "I guess you have his opinion on the subject then. But I agree, saving his life is the most important thing." He reached up and lovingly stroked Bodhi's forehead and told him, "My parents send their love too, man, and they said they're praying for you."

There was no indication from Bodhi that he'd registered a thing.

"We'll do our best for your friend," the doctor said. "Visiting hours are ending in a few minutes and they start up again at 8:00 am, so you should both probably go get some rest." He turned to leave and then stopped, turning back toward them. "If you're worried about him during the night, the nurses can keep you updated. Just be sure to get the 4-digit access code to his information before you leave. That way you won't have to keep explaining who you are."

* * *

Cooper and Ivy decided that they would be back to the hospital at the very moment visiting hours began the next morning. Nothing was going to keep them from Bodhi's side. They fell into bed beside each other, exhausted and worried.

As expected, Cooper couldn't sleep well. He called the hospital twice during the night, though they couldn't give him any concrete information. He also called before they left the hotel. "He's not any worse," he reported to Ivy. "That's a good thing." He'd tried to sound upbeat, but she saw through his charade. He was worried sick.

They rushed to Bodhi's bed and took up their stations on either side. Both of them had to touch him before they lost it. "Bodhi?" Ivy asked softly. "Are you awake? Can you hear me?"

Outside of an eye twitch, they didn't get much response. But then they simultaneously realized that Bodhi's hands were sweaty, and his brow looked damp. The shaking had ceased. "I think his fever's finally breaking!" Cooper whispered triumphantly. It was almost too good to believe. He punched the button to call the nurse. And sure enough, as soon as the nurse shooed them out of her way and scanned Bodhi's forehead, she announced happily, "His fever's down to 100.8. That's a huge improvement. I'll let Dr. Burton know right away."

Cooper dropped back into his chair and leaned over Bodhi. Ivy was already snuggled into Bodhi's side, so Cooper leaned into the pillow next to his head. Both of them draped their arms carefully over Bodhi's chest. They sat there immobile for a while until a soft, melodious voice broke the silence.

"If love could cure my son, I'm glad to see he's getting plenty of it from you two," said an attractive woman who'd just swept into the room wearing a gauzy floral skirt and a linen top. She was followed closely by a tall, handsome gentleman dressed in a delightfully gaudy Hawaiian shirt. They both had healthy tans, but their clothes looked rumpled, and their eyes were puffy from lack of sleep. There was no mistaking the dimpled chin on the man's face that was a carbon copy of Bodhi's. The woman's sparkling hazel eyes were also quite Bodhi-like.

Ivy's head popped up, and she smiled at the couple whom she instantly adored. She stood and held out her hand. "Hi, Mr. and Mrs. Monaghan, I'm Ivy."

Bodhi's mom engulfed her in a slightly plumeria-scented hug, and Ivy couldn't resist breathing in the clean floral perfume. "I'm so glad to meet you finally, Ivy. Call us Peach and Emmett, please."

Cooper and Emmett were clapping each other on the back with a bro-hug as the women acquainted themselves. Cooper stepped back and spoke up then, announcing, "We think he's doing better this morning!" He lowered his voice and continued, "I don't mind saying, last night it was pretty scary."

Just then, the nurse came in and said, "Only two visitors at a time, please." She made a hurry-up motion with her hand. "The other two of you can go wait down the hall."

Grabbing Cooper's hand, Ivy scooted him toward the door, saying to Peach and Emmett, "We'll let you both have some time with him then."

Looking at the retreating back of the nurse, Cooper whispered, "Doesn't that woman ever go home?"

Her head snapped toward them, and she barked, "Double shift." Then she stomped down the hallway away from them.

Chapter Twenty-Seven

As his temperature reached normal and stayed there, Bodhi's life was deemed out of danger. After some more careful observation, he was moved out of intensive care and into a regular room. All four of his guardian angels could hover over him at the same time this way, if they wanted. However, both couples acknowledged the need for personal time with the man they adored, so the visiting sessions ended up more like alternating shifts.

Emmett and Peach checked into the same hotel as Cooper and Ivy, and they all had a good laugh about the décor. It was easier, they reasoned, to all be together and it was close to the hospital. It also gave them time to get more acquainted when they weren't worrying over Bodhi at the hospital.

Bodhi looked happier and seemed to be delighted to see his parents, but he was still in pain. He remained uncharacteristically subdued for the first couple of days and tended to sleep a lot. At one point, however, when all four of his guests were crowding around him, he asked everyone, "Would you all mind, please? I'd really love to have a private word with Ivy."

Without delay, Emmett, Peach, and Cooper said they'd all go grab some coffee in the waiting area. As they exited the room, Ivy and Bodhi could hear Peach extolling the virtues of Kona coffee. "You really can't get the good stuff on the mainland," she explained as they made their way out.

Ivy's face crinkled up with worry as Bodhi reached out for her hand. "Come closer. And don't look so nervous." His voice rasped with lack of use.

Ivy sat down and stared at him. She waited.

"When I was really sick, I felt like I was inside a long tunnel, and it was so hard to see the other end. It was like looking for a tiny speck of light, and sometimes I couldn't even find it."

"Oh, Bodhi..." she sniffled. That sounded scary and awful to her.

He interrupted, "But even when the light went out, I heard things. Lots and lots of things. I just couldn't make myself respond. It was almost like being paralyzed; I had no strength to speak up."

"You did speak up a couple of times, though," she protested. "I heard you."

"I did? Sorry, I don't remember. Was it anything important?"

"Well, once you said you felt horrible and the other time you kind of told off the doctor for considering amputation." Ivy cringed.

Bodhi grunted and looked at the ceiling. "Some of what I heard scared the crap out of me." He caught her eye again. "But some of it was beautiful." Squeezing her hand weakly, he said, "I'm sorry for everything I've put you through, Ivy."

"I'm over it."

He finally gave her a real smile. "So, I heard. You love me after all."

"Yes." She locked onto his eyes. "I'm in love with you. I'm sorry I didn't admit it sooner. So, let's make a pact, okay?" He gave her a look. "No more apologies. No more reasons for apologies from here on out."

"But I've put you through hell."

"And I'm over it, Bodhi. Does knowing that work for you?"

"It does. It *so* does. You have no idea..."

Ivy leaned in and gave him a kiss. Pulling back, she said, "I'll say it again. I love you, Bodhi Monaghan. And I love Cooper. Cooper loves you. It's the perfect triad. We'll make it work."

Bodhi's doctor picked that moment to come to check him out. With a relieved smile, he said, "I think you're safely out of the woods now. It's a credit to your age and your general pre-injury health that we got this resolved so quickly. Would you like to go home?"

With a huge grin, Bodhi said, "Damn straight."

"Let's see how well you can do walking around, and if you can manage, I'll sign your discharge papers. You can be out of here in an hour or so."

Slowly, Bodhi sat up and swung his legs over the side of the bed. He'd been up a couple of times to get to the restroom, and knew he could do it with crutches. It was just a whole lot slower than he'd like, and his leg ached horribly. His head spun with the sudden motion.

"Easy, Bodhi." Ivy grabbed for him as he swayed.

"I'm fine," he protested.

"That's the attitude that got you here in the first place. Just take it one step at a time," she ordered.

When Bodhi made it to his feet, the doctor told him, "I'd like to see that you can make it down the hall to the double doors and back. It's fine to use the crutches. If that goes okay, I'll sign your papers."

Ivy realized Bodhi's butt was exposed in typical hospital gown fashion, so she grabbed the flimsy robe they'd provided and helped him into it. As much as she appreciated looking at him, she didn't feel much like sharing the view.

Bodhi swayed a bit again and smiled proudly as Cooper, his mom, and his dad breezed into the room.

"He's up!" Peach beamed happily.

Dr. Burton interjected, "We're just checking his overall strength before I cut him loose and send him home. I take it he has someone who can help him get around for the next few days?" He looked pointedly at Ivy, who nodded happily at the same time as Cooper rushed to Bodhi's free side. Cooper grasped his arm with a solid grip.

Smiling even more happily, Bodhi assured the doctor, "I have the best support a man could have." He turned to Ivy and kissed her soundly on the lips, then turned to Cooper and did the same.

Peach gave a happy little gasp and announced, "I *knew* it!"

Bodhi beamed at her and asked, "You're not upset?"

"Upset that you have not only one, but two gorgeous souls who love you to pieces? I'd be the biggest idiot and hypocrite in the world if I objected to that." She looked at Emmett. He was also smiling, but didn't say anything.

"Well, okay then," chuckled Dr. Burton. "Let's see how you do walking, shall we? I see you have a pair of those lovely hospital-issued slipper socks on already, so... whenever you're ready."

* * *

It took a while, but Bodhi passed the test, and they all decided to ride back to Del Mar together in Cooper's car. Emmett and Peach seemed all too happy to stick around rather than heading back to Maui.

"You can stay with us," announced Bodhi. "The hotels are pretty booked up during Del Mar's racetrack season, but we have a spare room."

On the drive home, Peach admitted to everyone, "I think Emmett and I have had our fill of the island life. We can play golf year-round just as easily in California. It will be more fun

—and more important in the long run—to be closer to family."
She looked fondly at her son who smiled back at her happily.

"That would be great, Mom."

"I will miss the coffee, though," she joked.

"We'll rent a car and start looking at property right away," Emmett declared. "Does anyone know a good realtor?"

Chapter Twenty-Eight

The first couple of days back home, Bodhi slept a lot. Then he progressed to getting up and walking short distances with the aid of one crutch. Deciding that cramped his style and looked dorky, he ditched the crutch and gritted his teeth when he went anywhere. He still had handfuls of antibiotics he needed to finish, so everyone watched him like a hawk to make sure he took all of his pills and had food handy to take them with.

Each day he felt better and grew stronger and stronger.

Cooper and Ivy alternated taking half days off from work at first. Bodhi's parents, although they chipped in to help with whatever they could do, spent a lot of time out looking at houses and trying to give the young people their privacy.

Each evening they all had dinner together, and Bodhi couldn't remember a more contented time in his entire life. He felt as though he were part of the large family he'd always dreamed of.

Two weeks after arriving in Del Mar, Emmett and Peach found a house they adored in Rancho Santa Fe. It was near the golf course and had, in Peach's words, "Just the right amount of space and yard for us, with plenty of room for when grandchildren come to play."

This made Ivy blush.

Cooper's eyebrows flew up.

Bodhi laughed and said, "Alright! Sounds great!"

Emmett submitted an offer, and it was accepted, so he decided to take them all out to dinner to celebrate. After a round of happy toasts, he said, "Now we'll have to head back to Maui for a while to get the other house sold and ship whatever we want back here. Those properties are in huge demand, so it ought to be a piece of cake."

Peach added, "I can't wait to get back in touch with some of our friends around here and let them know we're back again for good." Her eyes sparkled with delight. "Hawaii was a fun little adventure, but frankly we were getting island fever."

Ivy got an eager look on her face and said, "If you need any help decorating the new house, my friend Casey is an amazing designer. Actually, I can't wait for everyone to meet him." She winked at Cooper and Bodhi.

Two days later, they all hugged and said, "See you soon!" as the Monaghans left to fly back to Hawaii. They planned to move into their new place immediately upon their return.

"Privacy at last!" cried Bodhi the moment his parents' airport-bound Uber was out of sight. "I loved having them here, but I'll love it even more when they aren't sleeping right down the hall." He winked at Cooper, asking, "Anyone up for a *nap?*" He wiggled his eyebrows at Ivy. "Now that I don't have to worry about you two being so loud in bed…"

Cooper snorted. "Right. And you're Marcel Marceau."

"Are you well enough?" asked Ivy.

"Get serious. I have blue balls from all this forced celibacy. Let's have some fun!" He smacked them both playfully on their butts and pointed them toward the bedroom.

When they all got into the bedroom, Bodhi started to get undressed, but he noticed Cooper had plunked himself onto the bed with a funny look on his face, and he wasn't moving. "Coop? Something wrong, man?" Bodhi asked. Ivy stopped her disrobing and looked at Cooper as well.

With his brows slightly furrowed, Cooper took a moment. Finally, he said, "I need to get something off my chest." He noticed the worried look on Ivy's face and reached for her. "Come closer," he told her. "You too, Bodhi." Once he had both of them clasped in his hands, he continued, "Maybe this doesn't have to be spelled out, but..." He looked Bodhi straight in the eye. "You both know I was worried that you'd sweep back into town and somehow take over and I'd lose Ivy to you. I also worried you would just leave again; I couldn't let myself believe you might be here to stay. I couldn't stand either of those ideas, so at first I told myself that we were up for some sexy games that we'd somehow turn off when Ivy and I got married. Well, I don't want that at all, and I believe you're not going anywhere, Bodhi. I want this relationship—this triad of ours— to be permanent. And exclusive. I love what we have, and I hope we can sustain it forever. This is it for me." He looked at Ivy, "I still want to marry you, of course, but somehow I need for it to include Bodhi. Always. Are you up for that?"

Ivy gave him a glorious smile and said, "It sounds perfect, Cooper. I want us all to be happy." She looked at Bodhi. "We were so scared when you were sick, and it made us crazy with worry that we might lose you. I realized then just how deeply in love both Cooper and I were with you. You know I love you, but I also love that Cooper feels the same way about you as I do."

Bodhi's smile lit up the room, but for once words seemed to fail him. Instead, he bent down and kissed Cooper sweetly and gently for a moment, and then with more and more passion as his desire for the man grew. Pulling away finally, he kissed Ivy the same way, and then turned his attention once more to Cooper's mouth.

Watching her men make out always turned Ivy on. She felt an enormous swell of desire jolt through her so quickly, she had to squeeze her legs together. But when Bodhi whispered to Cooper, "I need to fuck your sweet ass today," she almost detonated with a long, keening groan.

Ivy and Bodhi stood in front of Cooper and began to take his clothes off. Cooper sat quietly as one piece of clothing after another disappeared. Bodhi kept up a monologue, saying, "I'm going to enjoy feeling my dick inside of you finally. I've been dreaming about this moment for months and months. And you're going to love it, Coop. It feels incredible, especially when your own cock is inside of Ivy at the same time."

"Well, um…" Ivy started. They looked at her with interest. "I love the idea of Cooper being in the middle, but can we try another new thing too?"

Cooper raised his eyebrows in question and Bodhi asked, "What's that?"

Ivy blushed and answered in a soft voice, "I want to feel what you guys feel. I know I don't have a prostate, but I'm curious about anal with a dick instead of a dildo or a plug, so, instead of my pussy…"

Cooper got a big grin and said, "Bring on the lube, babe! Of course."

So, they lay on the bed and formed a daisy chain of hands and asses, spreading lube into bottoms and murmuring soothing words to each other to encourage relaxing. Then for some reason, Bodhi started to snicker.

"What's so funny?" Ivy asked.

Bodhi tried to school his voice into seriousness and said, "I just want you both to know that I salute your bravery and sense of exploration, especially since I'm about to 'boldly go where no man has gone before!'"

The laughter that followed helped them all relax, and Cooper positioned Ivy in front of him as he lubed up his weeping erection. He couldn't remember ever being this turned on. He was about to fulfill two personal fantasies at the same time.

"Help her out a little, okay?" he asked Bodhi. Bodhi got in front of her and latched his mouth onto her clit as Cooper slowly and carefully eased himself into Ivy. She gasped and squirmed until she felt an orgasm building and building.

Sensing her impending release, Cooper encouraged her, "Let it go, babe." And she did.

Bodhi upped his pressure on her clit and sucked her over and over into his mouth until she stilled. Then, not being able to stand it a minute longer, he hopped off the bed and got behind Cooper again. Spreading Cooper's ass cheeks apart, he admired the view for a moment, applied another squirt of lube, and then carefully entered his friend.

"Holy...!" cried Cooper. He sucked in a massive gulp of air.

"You okay, buddy?" Bodhi asked with concern.

"I'm... fine. When did you get such a big dick, though? Fuck!" Cooper gradually relaxed and grew accustomed to the amazing sensations both fore and aft while Ivy and Bodhi laughed with him happily.

Cooper didn't last much longer. He felt Ivy stiffening in his arms and reached down to play with her nub as she had another ear-splitting orgasm. That set him off, and he bellowed out in relief as a colossal buzz of pure erotic delight launched through him. Bodhi took a bit longer as he relished the feel of Cooper's tight backside. Pulsing with ecstasy, he thrust in and out in a frenzy until he filled Cooper with a stream of ejaculate. Bodhi saw stars behind his closed eyelids.

Cooper was the first to speak up. "Right now, I feel like 'God's in his heaven and all's right with the world.'"

Ivy raised her head and looked at her men. "You guys are full of pithy quotes today," she chuckled.

"Care to add one?" Bodhi asked with a lazy grin.

"Hmm... I can't think of any right now, but I will say that that was more fun than a barrel of monkeys." She giggled at their groans. "Let's go take a shower, you guys. We're all lube-y and cummy."

Chapter Twenty-Nine

Ivy was so bolstered by their incredible sex-capades the day before, she asked over breakfast, "I'd like us all to get together with Casey and his husband and wife. Are you two up for it? I'm sure you guys will like them, and it would be interesting to visit with more people in a triad."

"Sure," answered Cooper.

Bodhi nodded and said, "Sounds great. See if you can set something up. And, by the way, you can both stop babysitting me now. I'm fine and I need to get back to work as badly as the both of you do. I have investments that need my attention, and I still have to extricate myself from the lease on the London apartment and get some stuff shipped here." He looked fondly at Cooper then Ivy and added, "I can't tell you both how much your help and support meant to me while I was a mess." He reached out and grasped their hands. "I love you both so much. I guess I just had to leave and go through a bit of hell to fully appreciate what I had right in front of me all along."

Cooper got a thoughtful look on his face and asked, "Do you think we'd have actually ever gotten here if you'd stayed, though?" He looked at their doubtful expressions. "I wonder if we'd have ever pushed the envelope or if we'd all have suffered in silence. I was so jealous of both of you, it was driving me crazy."

"And here, all that time I felt awful knowing I was in love with Bodhi and desperately attracted to his hot best friend,"

Ivy interjected. "I thought there had to be something wrong with me that I couldn't control my... I don't know... libido or urges or something."

Bodhi smiled at them ruefully. "I didn't have a clue how to deal with my feelings either. I was in love with two amazing people at the same time but instead of being honest about it—even to myself—I freaked out and ran away like an idiot," he muttered. "Not my finest moment."

"Well, we're here now, and it's great." Cooper looked at Ivy and asked, "When are you going to talk to Casey?"

"I can call him right now, actually." Smiling, she went to retrieve her phone. As she reentered the kitchen where they were all finishing their coffee, she was already on the phone with her friend, saying, "Oh! Um, well... sure. That would be terrific. Tomorrow night?" She looked toward her men with raised eyebrows and grinned when they both nodded. "Seven? Perfect." She listened for a moment and widened her eyes. "Oh, you don't have to do that, we can drive ourselves... Well in that case, I'll text you the address. Thanks, Casey! I wasn't calling to wrangle an invitation for all of us, but if you say your chef is as good as all that, we'll bring our appetites." She laughed and smiled some more. "We'll be there. Thanks a lot. I look forward to meeting Willa and Jackson, and the guys are both anxious to meet all of you too."

After she hung up, she explained that Casey and his family had moved out of their La Jolla beach house because it was being rebuilt, and they were living in his estate out in Rancho Santa Fe.

"They don't all live together?" Bodhi asked.

"No, it's not that. They do all live together, but Jackson and Willa were originally next-door neighbors in La Jolla, and now they're tearing down those two houses and building one big beach house. Casey still has this incredible place in Rancho that they use when they want more privacy. He's been raving about his chef Phillipe for the longest time, so he says he wants to show him off. Casey loves to be social, so as soon as I said the words 'get together' he planned the whole thing. He's sort of like a force of nature. Oh, and they're sending us a car and driver."

* * *

The next evening, they were delighted to see a limousine pull up to their house right on time. A uniformed driver climbed out and explained, "Mr. Mitchell and Mr. Melrose like to make sure their friends get home safely after a dinner party."

"Mr. Mitchell?" asked Bodhi.

"Sorry, I should have explained, Bodhi," Ivy said. "Casey's husband and lifelong friend is Jackson Mitchell—you know, the inventor of Face-to-Face."

"Oh... *that* Mr. Mitchell. Cool." Bodhi's grin was nearly ear-to-ear and his smile looked even more dazzling than usual because he'd shaved off his beard. His captivating chin dimple showed itself once again—much to the delight of his two lovers.

Admiring Bodhi's handsome face, Ivy added, "Wait until you guys see this house. I went to a party there before I met you, and it was magnificent. Casey's taste is impeccable."

* * *

Casey's family proved to be as charming and welcoming to them as if they were all long-lost friends. Jackson greeted them with a toddler in his arms whom he introduced as Matilda.

Willa, a gorgeous, down-to-earth blonde vision, who was visibly pregnant again, gave everyone a hug. And Casey seemed to be in his element entertaining everyone. They started with a tour of the grounds around the property. He'd been adding on lately. The acreage now included another beautiful—though smaller—house where he explained that Chef Phillipe and his wife Gabrielle lived.

"A live-in chef with his own house sounds like a pretty good deal," observed Bodhi.

"Phillipe is more than our chef. He's like part of the family now. Not... part of the triad," Casey explained. "So don't get the wrong idea. But we love having him and his wife around, and this way he doesn't have to commute to work."

After drinks and chatting, they all sat down at an enormous table. Phillipe joined them, asking them to excuse his wife's tardiness. "She'll be along soon. She got held up with an international call."

Ivy blinked and asked, "What kind of work does she do?"

Casey snorted. "Monkey business!" The guests eyed him quizzically.

Just then they heard the unmistakable sound of a helicopter nearby that seemed to be landing somewhere on the property.

Jackson, in response to their surprised looks, explained, "It cuts down on Gabrielle's commute time to San Diego. We've started using helicopters a lot recently."

About a minute later, a petite brunette flitted into the room muttering rapid apologies in French. She rushed into the waiting arms of Phillipe who kissed her soundly and then stood back, still holding her hand. "Everyone, this is my Gabrielle. She's a primate curator at the San Diego Zoo."

After introductions were made, a several-person wait staff proceeded to take care of serving them dinner. When Casey noticed the thinly-veiled looks of surprise on Ivy and her men's faces at all of the servants, he laughed and announced,

"We don't want to overburden Phillipe, so we're sort of like Down-to-earth Abbey around here." Then he cracked up at his own joke as Phillipe rolled his eyes. "He has enough to do with the meal planning, shopping, and cooking, and the rest of us are busy with our own work. Willa, as you all probably know, is an amazing author and has a movie that's coming out soon, and Jackson is inventing the next revolutionary app."

Matilda took that moment to fling something resembling mashed potatoes. It landed with a splat next to Casey's plate. He laughed even harder and said, "And we all have babies to raise and babies to make." He stood and picked up his daughter, snuggling and kissing her until she giggled. Then he sat her down again and said, "We don't throw food, young lady." After that, Matilda behaved.

They may have a large staff of servants, but it was obvious to everyone that there was a relaxed atmosphere and a lot of love to go around in this house.

At about the same time as they finished dinner, Matilda slumped over and fell asleep, so Willa excused herself to put the little girl to bed. "I'll meet you all in the living room as soon as I can." She smiled at Jackson who'd popped up from his chair. He gently extricated Matilda from the highchair and offered her to Willa, kissing the little girl before he handed her off.

As Willa left with Matilda, Phillipe and Gabrielle said their goodnights to everyone, explaining they'd have dessert at home. They instinctively knew it was time to leave and took off holding hands—looking at each other with their hearts in their eyes.

During dinner, Jackson had learned that Bodhi handled investments, so they spent the rest of the meal deep in conversation about that. As they were finishing up dessert, Casey, Ivy, and Cooper got into a light-hearted conversation about remodeling houses to accommodate a triad rather than the traditional couple. "Have you guys ever heard of an Australian King bed?" Casey asked. When they shook their heads, he directed them to follow him down the hall. Guiding them into the master suite, he proudly indicated a bed that was roughly the size of Texas.

"Awesome!" Cooper exclaimed. "We'd need a bigger bedroom though." Then he added, "We already need a bigger garage."

Casey winked at him, and even though Cooper knew it wasn't flirtatious, the reality of knowing someone else who lived the life of a triad and was one hundred percent accepting of this lifestyle did all kinds of warm things to him inside.

Making their way back toward the library, they found Willa exiting Matilda's room with a warm, sleepy smile. She immediately took Ivy's arm and asked, "Would you like a private word?" Ivy felt relief flow through her, even though she hadn't been particularly aware of any tension prior to this. To the men, Willa said, "We'll be in the library for a few minutes and then we'll join you all in the living room."

Once they were seated in a gorgeous room that was large, though still had a feeling of intimacy, Willa addressed Ivy's concerns head-on. "I know you have a million questions, and I'm here for you if you need to ask. I'll make sure you have my cell number if you ever want to talk. We have a lot in common, Ivy." She smiled at her warmly. "And, in a practical sense..." she stood and walked to one of the many bookshelves where she pulled out two brand-new hardback volumes with colorful jackets on them. "I'd like to give these to you." Ivy's eyes grew large as she realized they were copies of Willa's own books. The top one bore the title *The Passion of Three,* and it was obvious by the three people on the cover what the story was about. Laughing, Willa sat back down and said, "Before I met Jackson and Casey, I did a lot of research into polyamory and wrote these books. They're based on my imagination but also some interviews and some diligent research. Once I entered into the triad with Casey and Jackson, however, I stopped writing books in this sub-genre. I may go back to them at a later date, but for now I'm focusing on more traditional relationship stories."

"Why?"

Willa smiled and answered, "I don't want people thinking that everything I write is autobiographical and they're seeing into my bedroom at night. We've had enough scrutiny in that area because of that horrible couple who posted the video of us."

Ivy made an understanding face. "That must have been so terrible," she said.

"It was," Willa replied. "But at the same time, it meant we had to face who we were to each other, head-on. We love our family the way it is and don't need to answer to anyone or get anyone's approval."

Ivy looked down at the books, saying, "Thank you for these. I guess they may give us some... ideas?"

"Precisely," Willa laughed. "Do you have any questions before we go back and meet up with our men?"

Ivy pondered a moment and then asked, "How do you keep things fair? I worry about jealousies and competitiveness. I know it's not all up to me, but..." She trailed off as Willa got a knowing look in her eyes.

"Jackson, bless his heart, has been the one who's had to work on that the most with our relationship. He's such a beautiful, giving man with a generous spirit that you cannot believe, but I know at first things were hard for him. He wanted this to happen, and it never would have without his organizing it, but there was still this sense that he not only knew me before Casey did, he knew Casey before I did. The dynamics had to change a little in his head before he was completely comfortable."

Ivy nodded. "Sounds kind of like Bodhi. He likes to take charge. Cooper and I secretly love it, but we won't tell him that. He likes to think he's controlling things." She gave a soft chuckle.

"Ivy, the important thing to remember, if I can give you one piece of advice, is that the balance of power and levels of affection are fluid in any relationship. In a triad, that means three people's feelings and power dynamics instead of two. Pay attention to not slighting anyone, but don't obsess over it. There's no big scorecard you need to follow. If you love your men, let them see it and know it constantly. You'll all be fine."

"Thank you, Willa." Ivy looked perplexed and blurted, "How am I supposed to tell my family? Cooper still wants to get married. Do I do that and just have Bodhi live with us? Is that fair to Bodhi? Do I lie to my parents? I'm not all that close to them, and they live in Chicago, but they'll want to have some explanation if I say, 'Oh, by the way, I'm considering marrying two guys instead of one.'" She laughed and said, "Sorry... that was a lot all at once."

"Lying doesn't sound like too great of a plan. Jackson and Casey's families have been thrilled for us, so we never had any problems with that. I lost my parents..."

"Oh! I'm so sorry!"

"Thank you. I don't know how they'd have reacted, honestly. They were more traditional than Casey or Jackson's parents. But I also know I couldn't have kept them in the dark. Maybe your family will surprise you. If they don't, well, you have two wonderful men to keep you happy and warm at night."

Ivy nodded, but she still looked worried.

"Ready to go see what the guys are up to?" Willa asked.

Ivy stood, clutching her new books to her chest. "Yes. Thank you for these and for, well, listening and everything."

* * *

The men were all huddled around a laptop screen looking serious when the ladies found them. Cooper looked up as they entered the vast room and grinned at Ivy. "Casey has a solution!" he announced.

"What's the question?" asked Ivy.

"How we can *all* be married—more or less."

Ivy's eyebrows shot up. This was not what she'd expected. When she saw them crowded around the computer screen, she imagined a breaking news announcement or the score of some sports ball game. "Um...?"

Casey looked up and explained with a broad smile, "I'm going to get myself ordained. We found the site that authorizes it for the state of California. Cooper's law firm is going to draw up all the legal documents giving each of you the equivalent of spousal rights, and although Cooper and Ivy will be the ones who are married in the eyes of the law, I can also include Bodhi in the vows, worded in such a way that makes you all equal life partners to each other. Brilliant, yeah?"

All Ivy had to do was look at Bodhi and Cooper's happy faces to understand that they were satisfied with the solution. It bothered her a bit, though, so she asked, "Aren't you guys forgetting something important?"

Four sets of eyes stared at her in confusion.

Willa looked like she was about to burst out laughing at their perplexed faces. "You're all such a bunch of 'fix-it' guys." She cocked one eyebrow and nodded her head toward Ivy.

Ivy pursed her lips and got a mulish look on her face. She looked like she was about to tap her toe in annoyance. She also seemed to be holding back a fit of laughter, however. And a second later, when none of the men spoke up, she let it go. When she reined in her giggles at last, she exclaimed, "Hello! I'm here too. Was anyone going to ask me *my* opinion?"

Bodhi and Cooper stared at each other in mild horror, and both of them stepped toward Ivy. Cooper dropped to one knee and asked, "I know you and I are already engaged, but will you marry both of us?" at the same time that Bodhi dropped to a knee, grimaced in agony and popped back up again as he sucked in a pained moan.

"Sorry," he said grasping her free hand—whether in affection or to steady himself wasn't readily apparent. "I can't quite do the kneeling thing yet. Ivy Chambers, will you do Cooper and me the honor of marrying both of us?" Then he turned to Cooper and asked, "Will you marry Ivy and me?"

Of course, everyone said yes, yes, yes, and Casey summoned a bottle of champagne for them to toast the new triad's official status.

Chapter Thirty

On the ride home, Ivy showed the guys the two books Willa had gifted her. Ivy and Bodhi poured over *Triple Cravings* while Cooper grabbed for *The Passion of Three* and started flipping through it looking for the "good parts." Quickly he said, "Look at this, you two. Do you think it's real? Can two guys actually do this with a woman? Holy shit!" He pointed to a paragraph and set the book onto Ivy's lap.

Ivy answered, "Willa assured me that she'd done lots of research into it, and she also interviewed people. So, I believe if she says it happens, it happens." She lowered her voice. "Besides, it sounds amazing!"

Bodhi and Cooper looked at her in awe. Then they looked at each other. Bodhi had to adjust himself, and Cooper was blushing like crazy. He cleared his throat and said, "Well! Okay, then. Willa should know."

"She also told me she wrote these books before they started their triad, and she's taking a break now from writing them—sort of a privacy thing so readers won't think she's being autobiographical."

"I wish the driver would go faster," whispered Bodhi. "Do you think he would if I tipped him?" They all snickered. "Oh! Speaking of money and tips, I need to tell you both something fantastic that happened." He had their full attention, so he continued. "Jackson asked me to email him a contract so

I can *manage his investments*. Can you help me draw one up, Cooper?"

Cooper happily agreed.

Bodhi beamed. "This is going to be incredible! Jackson and I really hit it off, and he has quite the talent for making money. I probably won't need any other clients with his billion-plus business and my own investments. Pretty soon we can move into a bigger house!"

"With room for kids?" Ivy asked.

"Lots of them," he laughed. "Coop, are you on board with this?"

"Definitely. I can't let my sisters be the only grandchild producers in the family."

* * *

As soon as they closed the front door, clothes began to disappear. They left a trail of fabric leading all the way from the foyer to the master bedroom. Laughing and kissing each other, they made their way clumsily down the hall as they climbed out of each pair of pants or whisked a shirt over their heads. Shoes were discarded in a jumble, and finally undergarments landed on the floor beside the bed.

"I think it's Lady's Choice Night," announced Bodhi. "Would the lady prefer page two hundred and eleven in *Triple Cravings* or one hundred and six in *The Passion of Three*?" He gave Ivy a lecherous grin.

Ivy seemed to ponder her choices a moment and then answered, "Two eleven sounds good for tonight. I'd like to save the other for our wedding night, if it's okay with you guys." Then she burst out laughing. Sobering for a moment she added, "Speaking of weddings, I guess I need to call my parents pretty soon."

Cooper nuzzled her neck saying, "That may be true, but there's no room for parents in the bedroom tonight. I'll grab some lube."

Bodhi was already massaging and kissing Ivy's tatas with loving care as she purred her approval.

Cooper returned and locked lips with Ivy. He wound his arms around her and stroked her body at the same time as he caressed what he could reach of Bodhi. The sight of Bodhi's mouth on her nipples was a huge turn-on, so he leaned down and gave the breast that Bodhi had just vacated the same treatment as his buddy was giving to the other.

Ivy squirmed as she felt large male hands reach down and caress her most sensitive parts. Cooper toyed with her clit and slowly plunged a finger inside her at the same time that Bodhi began to circle her puckered entrance. Bodhi pulled away for a moment and returned to her body with a well-lubed finger that he slid carefully in and out of her. He simultaneously nibbled her breast and bit down lightly on her nipple. She gasped at the sensation, and he slid a second finger into her.

"Ohmygawd, you guys! If this is what it feels like to be in the middle, no wonder you two like it so much." Cooper sped up his hand against her clit and increased the pressure until her legs almost gave out and she cried, "Yes! Oh, yesss." She shuddered as spasm after spasm rocked her so hard, she had to hold onto Cooper's shoulders for support.

He removed his hand and said, "Bodhi, I think it would be best if you lie down on the bed and I'll ease Ivy onto you. That'll be the easiest position for your leg."

"I'm fine," Bodhi assured them for what felt like the millionth time. They just smirked at him, so he flopped down spread-eagle in the middle of the bed. "Bring it on," he exclaimed and shuddered with delight.

Cooper and Ivy hopped onto the bed on either side of him, and Ivy reached for his erection. Cooper, however, was faster to lean in and engulfed Bodhi in his mouth. As he went after Bodhi with enthusiasm, Ivy grabbed the lube and greased up her finger. Bodhi writhed and moaned as Cooper sucked him down over and over, and Ivy toyed with his balls and then slide her finger into Bodhi's tight backside.

Finally Bodhi cried, "Stop! I want to come inside Ivy with you, Coop. You have to stop. This feels too good."

Cooper removed his mouth with a satisfied grin and squirted a generous amount of lube onto Bodhi's red, pulsing dick. He rubbed it up and down until Bodhi began to squirm. "Please, I need Ivy now," Bodhi begged.

Cooper then positioned Ivy in front of him and lubed up her butt some more. He kissed her back and neck as he made her ready for Bodhi. When she nodded that she was relaxed enough, he helped her get into place over Bodhi's body, facing away from him.

Bodhi relished the view as Cooper supported Ivy and she lowered herself onto his cock. Her ass was so tight, he had to concentrate on not coming before things really got started. Her little mewling noises of pleasure-pain almost did him in, however. Finally, she was seated to the hilt.

Cooper took up the position in front of Ivy then and slid his massive erection into her pussy. Ivy cried out, startling them both. "Are you alright?" Cooper asked her.

"This feels... *incredible*," she breathed, barely able to articulate the words.

As Cooper began to shove himself in and out, Bodhi reached around Ivy to play with her clit. "It feels amazing," he whispered in awe. "Ivy, you're like a vise on my dick, and I can feel Cooper rubbing against me. Have I died and gone to heaven?"

Ivy chuckled at him and said, "If it is, I'm right there with you. I never in my life thought this would feel as great as it does."

Cooper sped up his motions and croaked through clenched teeth, "Is anyone else about to come? I don't know how long I can keep this up. It's... so... Ohmygawd."

Ivy soon realized she could squeeze her muscles and make Bodhi moan and shake. So, she continued to do it in time with Cooper's thrusts. But everything felt so over-the-top sensual, she was the first to succumb to her orgasm. She cried out as pleasure stabbed through her over and over, and that set Bodhi off with a shout. Cooper joined them at last, wrapping his arms around Ivy and shaking with his release.

When Cooper and Ivy took their places on the bed on either side of Bodhi, no one spoke for a moment as they each felt their hearts pound. Ivy eventually said, "Just think, guys. We can have this much fun for the rest of our lives." That set off a chain reaction of kissing each other until they headed to the shower.

Chapter Thirty-One

Several days later, Ivy knew that the time had come to address her parents. But how? *Good question*, she thought to herself. Over breakfast, she asked the guys, "Do you have any suggestions?"

Cooper was the first to reply, and he answered, "We don't know them, babe, but I'd just go for the old 'rip off the band-aid' approach and get it over with, if it were me."

"I might ease into it somehow," Bodhi countered. "But my parents were cool about it. You saw them. And Cooper's family accepted the idea as soon as he told them too. Maybe you're worried about nothing."

"You're forgetting that your families already knew you guys and had a good sense of what was going on probably long before the two of you admitted it to yourselves." The guys looked at each other with mild surprise. "My family hasn't been around us at all. They might be scandalized."

Bodhi cleared his throat and shrugged his shoulder. "What's the worst that could happen?"

"They might refuse to speak to me ever again."

"Yeah... so?" He looked her in the eye. "I don't mean to sound cold, but if they can't accept us the way we are, would you *want* to speak to them? Do they have a history of homophobia or something?"

Cooper smiled sadly at them and said, "Bodhi's right. I know they're your family, but you haven't seen them in over two years. It's not as if you'll expect them to move next door and babysit someday."

Ivy looked back and forth between her men. She was suddenly a nervous wreck. "I don't remember them ever being homophobic. In fact, I have a gay cousin, and they've been fine about him. But... I'm their daughter, you know? Maybe they'll have a different standard they expect for me."

Bodhi got an irritated look on his face and asked, "Are *you* fine with us?"

"Of course I am!"

"Hmm." He looked at Cooper, who had an inscrutable expression on his face. "I think Coop's right then. Just rip that ol' bandage right off and get it over with. You're buying trouble by waiting. We'll be here for you, no matter what happens." He looked pointedly at her phone that sat next to her coffee on the table.

Ivy stood, jumped up and down a couple of times, cranked her neck from side to side, shook her hands out, and took a deep breath like she was about to compete in an Olympic event.

"Is that helping?" asked Cooper who looked like he was trying not to laugh.

She huffed at him and announced, "I am not responsible for anything my mother says, okay?" She sat back down, scooted her phone in front of her and commanded, "Hey, Siri, call Mom and Dad." Ivy immediately put it on speaker as they all heard it ring.

"Hello?" said a feminine voice after the third ring.

"Hi, Mom. How are you and Dad doing? I'm here with—"

"Ivy, sweetie! It's good to hear from you. It's been a while. We're fine. Your dad's knee's been bothering him after he plays tennis, but other than that, we're doing great. I think he needs to lose a few pounds and that knee of his would stop hurting." They heard an audible sigh. "I had a call just yesterday from your sister. She's... well, I think maybe she needed some money, and that's why she called. She's always been bad with budgeting—not like you at all. We were just bragging about you and your successful gallery to our friends Janie and Thomas, remember them? We had dinner together last week and they said to tell you hello..." The woman seemed able to talk without taking a breath. It would have been impressive, Ivy thought, if it weren't so maddening.

Finally, Ivy interrupted her. "*Mom*, I'm getting married."

"Well, yes, sweetie, you told me that a few months ago, and we couldn't be happier. Have you finally decided on a date? Are you going to bring Cooper home to meet us one of these days? What kind of color scheme do you think you might want to have? Shall I look into reserving the country club for the reception? I'll need to check to see when St. Paul's is available for the service too. It's much nicer than St. Luke's. The church is always in demand, so I probably need to know a window of possible dates. There's also always All Saints but I don't really—"

"Mom, please slow down. I'm pretty sure we're all getting married here in California, not in Chicago. And you should know I'm on the phone here with—"

"*All?*" she interrupted loudly. "Whatever are you talking about, Ivy? Are you thinking of having a double wedding with a friend? Those sound like fun, but I've never been to one I liked. It takes too much of the attention off the bride, and it's *your* special day, after all. You only get married once—if you're lucky, of course—and it ought to be perfect..."

Ivy looked at Bodhi and Cooper who were turning red in the face as they tried to be quiet and not laugh at Ivy's frustration over her mother's stream of consciousness delivery. She took a deep breath and interrupted, "I'm not having a double wedding with a friend. *I'm marrying two men.*"

There was complete silence on the other end of the conversation.

That was a first.

"Mom, remember when I told you about Bodhi—Cooper's best friend and roommate?"

"That awful man who broke your heart? What about him?"

Bodhi immediately studied the contents of his coffee mug as if it held the secrets of the universe.

"Mom! Bodhi's not awful at all. He's been back from England now for quite a while, and we've... um... made up our differences. He's actually quite an exceptional person. He, Cooper, and I all live together now, and we're all happy."

"Are you sure?" her mother asked in a shaky voice. "I don't want you to get hurt again. And I certainly don't want to think of you servicing two men at the same time. I think you ought to have more self-respect than that, young lady. What do they do—trade you back and forth?"

"Mom! They're here on speakerphone with me."

Another shocked silence. Two in one phone call. It was a family record. "Well, you could have warned me, you know," Ivy's mother chastised.

"I was trying to, but you kept interrupting me."

"I never—!"

Cooper couldn't stand it; he had to butt in. "Mrs. Chambers, this is Cooper. I want to assure you that Ivy's self-respect is something Bodhi and I value. I'm sure as well as you do. We both love her with our whole hearts, but the fact is, Bodhi and I... um... also love each other. I hope you can accept that."

There was a loud gasp.

Bodhi spoke up then and said, "I'm here too, Mrs. Chambers. Cooper's right. We're an equal triad, and we've never been happier. I can't apologize enough for leaving the two of them when I was so messed up in the head about my feelings. I promise you, however, that Ivy *and* Cooper's happiness is the most important thing in the world to me."

"Well!" Ivy's mom exclaimed. "Ivy, dearest, are you certain this is what you want for your life? It's not just some strange thing they do out there in California, is it? It could just be a fad. My friend Linda's son went to San Francisco for art school, and he turned into a hippie!"

Ivy began to laugh. "That was Ben, and he's become such a successful artist, I've had two different shows featuring his work in my gallery, Mom. He's a bit of an outlier in how he dresses, but I assure you, he's taken seriously for his talent." She rolled her eyes at her men. Then she got an idea. "Mom, I'm going to send you some information to read. It might give you a better idea of our commitment to each other. I'll email you later today, okay?"

"Well, I suppose. It's clear that whatever I say isn't going to make much of a difference. You're apparently more like your sister than I thought. She never listens to me at all and just look at the messes she's gotten herself into—"

"Mom."

"Just last week she was talking about adopting *another* dog from the shelter, and she already has three of them—"

"*Mom.*"

"Don't shout at me, Ivy."

"I'm sorry. It's just that we don't have all morning to discuss Holly's desire to adopt dogs. I just wanted to say that I love you and Dad, and I would like to know that you'll be here for the wedding."

"There's going to be a *wedding?* How on earth does that work for three people?"

"Don't worry. We'll work out the details, some of which will be only symbolic. Will you come? We don't have a date yet, but I'd love to know we have your blessing."

"Ivy... I'll have to speak to your father. This is really a bit much to take in, and I simply cannot imagine what he'll have to say about it. He's off playing tennis right now, and then he planned to get the car washed, so I hope he'll be back in time to get ready for our company. We're having a couple over who just moved in down the street, and they seem so nice." She gasped again. "What on earth can I tell them when they ask about our daughters?"

Ivy laughed and answered, "Tell them your older daughter Holly has a thing for stray dogs and your younger daughter Ivy is a sexual deviant."

"Ivy!"

"I'm just kidding, Mom. Tell them whatever you want. I'm sure you'll be able to figure it out." She looked at the guys' faces then and realized they were clearly stifling their laughter for her benefit. "I love you, Mom. I just have to go now and service my... I mean I have to go buy groceries."

Her mom was probably going to launch into a tirade about Ivy cooking and cleaning for two men, but the fact was, Ivy loved to cook and when she didn't feel like it, there was always take-out. They'd also recently hired a housekeeper to take care of the cleaning and laundry, so she said again, "Love you! Bye!" and she disconnected the call. She exhaled a long, cleansing breath. "Well, that went better than I expected, all things con-sidered," she told them, and they all burst out laughing.

* * *

Much later that night, Ivy received a breathless call from her mother.

"Ivy! You'll never believe this!"

"Hi, Mom. What's up?"

"You know the neighbors I told you about? The ones we had over this evening? It turns out that they have a son who is in a relationship with a woman and another couple! They told us all about it. It's called polyamory, in case you're wondering. They weren't embarrassed about it in the least. In fact, they were proud of their son and explained to us all about the philosophy or practice or whatever you want to call it of *compersion*. That's where you get pleasure from someone else's pleasure— like the opposite of jealousy. It sounds so lovely! He lives in Greenwich Village, so I guess that kind of thing goes on there. I think it's sort of like what we used to call swingers, but in this case there's more commitment. They told us *all about it!* I thought your father was going to have a heart attack at first, but then he calmed down and said maybe it was a good thing that people are trying new things. I don't know why he said that, but I couldn't keep my mouth shut, and I blurted out that you're in what you called a triad with two men you love, and do you know what they said? They said you're one helluva lucky woman!"

"What did Dad say?"

"Your father?"

"Yes!"

"Oh, um... he got kind of quiet, and it made me realize my timing wasn't exactly perfect, but he acted like he knew all about it then so he could save face. You know how he is. By the time our guests left, I think he was actually fine with it. I wasn't so sure at first, but he seems okay. He didn't say any-thing bad about it anyway. He went straight to bed after that because that darn knee was acting up again, so I'll talk to him about it again privately tomorrow, but I think he's fine, really. I just wanted to let you know that in today's circles apparently your lifestyle is enviable. I... well, I can't see it for myself, but if it makes you happy, then I say it's fine with me. I can't wait to tell Shannon and Marie." Her mom got the giggles then, and Ivy wondered if she may have been a teensy bit tipsy.

"Thanks for letting me know, Mom. I'm glad you approve, but I wasn't going to change things even if you didn't. You know that, right?"

"You always did have a mind of your own, sweetie. I'll say good night now."

"Bye, Mom. Love you."

"I love you too." She hung up giggling.

Chapter Thirty-Two

Many weeks later, the wedding guests rose to their feet and stood in front of Casey in the rearranged living room of his estate. The magnificent fireplace gave the room a warm glow, and candles flickered in strategic arrangements around the area. The men were all resplendent in their tuxedoes, and the woman wore gowns of jeweled tones. All of their families and close friends were there to share the joy of three people they all loved.

It had taken a while for Ivy's dad to be truly accepting of his daughter's chosen path, but after plenty of reflection he finally told his wife, "The world is changing so quickly. Some of it stinks but a lot of it is beautiful. I guess I need to let some of the rules we grew up with go and be happy for them. They really are great guys, aren't they?"

A string quartet was positioned in the back corner of the room, playing *Ode to Joy* as—with a proud smile on his handsome face—Ivy's father led his daughter toward Bodhi and Cooper. The delight emanating from them was infectious. When he reached the front, Mr. Chambers kissed Ivy and gave the grooms a stern, warning look that clearly conveyed his meaning that they'd better not mess up with his precious daughter.

The look made Casey chuckle to himself, and he instantly thought of how he'd react to Matilda marrying someday. He got it.

Rather than facing Casey in a row, they elected to join hands in a circle in front of him. Bodhi had suggested that this arrangement made sense to him as he felt he was marrying both Cooper and Ivy at the same time. The symbolism was not lost on the attendees as they settled back into their seats.

The music ended and Casey began, "The love of a triad is a special kind of love. It requires generosity, patience, plenty of communication, and sometimes a thick skin around the doubters of the world. Ivy, Bodhi, and Cooper have gone through their share of challenges, but more may still arise. Knowing them as I do, I'm sure they are up to facing their journey together as a unified force. I respect their bravery, and their tenacity, and the commitment it takes to set aside the easy route to take the more personal path that works for them—one that I'm sure you all know I wholeheartedly enjoy myself. In the famous words of Dr. Seuss, 'Oh, the places you'll go!'" He winked at Jackson and Willa who sat nearby and gave them a blinding smile. Soft laughter broke out, and as it faded away, he looked at the guests and asked, "Will everyone here make a promise right now to support Cooper, Bodhi, and Ivy emotionally in the years to come? If you agree, please say together, 'I promise.'"

"I promise!" rang out from every guest.

"I can only consecrate one union legally in the eyes of the State of California, and whether or not these three want to make it clear who is marrying whom is up to them. In actuality, however, all three are going forth as permanent life partners from today on, so the legal points are more or less moot."

The ceremony continued with a lovely song that Ivy's sister Holly sang, and finally Bodhi, Cooper, and Ivy pledged their troths to each other as life partners forever. Each of them had a ring for the others, which meant that they all wore two bands on their ring fingers. Ivy gave her men matching platinum bands, Bodhi and Cooper gave each other gold bands, and they both gave Ivy bands that were covered in a row of diamonds. They'd commissioned a talented jeweler who designed them in such a way that the rings nestled together perfectly on their fingers, making each set seem like one wedding band.

Casey addressed the crowd, "In as much as Ivy, Cooper, and Bodhi have consented to come together in wedlock and have witnessed the same before this company and pledged their vows to each other, by the authority vested in me by the State of California, I now pronounce two of you married. Whether the State of California condones it or not, I now pronounce you all husband, wife, and husband—all life partners. You may now all kiss each other."

Cheers and clapping erupted as the circle of newlyweds grew smaller. Clasped hands were dropped as arms wound around each other, and they exchanged kiss after kiss. Several hankies came out of pockets and purses when family and friends witnessed such unabashed and honest affection.

They partied for several hours before it was time to take off. Jackson had graciously loaned them one of his luxury Gulfstreams for their honeymoon trip. "My gift to you!" he'd announced, much to their delight and gratitude. The plan was to fly to Sydney, Australia where the guys could try out the surfing, and Ivy could scope out the art scene. She also planned to surf a little as the guys had been giving her lessons. She liked it, but not the way her men did. In any case, they had two weeks to enjoy the city and see as much as they could of New South Wales. They might even look at art for the new house that they were building.

Jackson's helicopter took them to the airport where they boarded the private jet. "This plane is amazing!" Ivy gushed as she took in the luxurious décor. It was naturally equipped with a stateroom that accommodated three with a large bed. Once they were airborne and the seatbelt caution was lifted, they all bolted for the bed and discarded their clothing at record speed.

"I can't believe we're all still awake," Cooper observed with a laugh. "It's been a long day. I'm not complaining, my dearest wife and husband, I hope you realize. This has been the best day of my life."

"And it's just going to get better," Bodhi said in a rumbling, deep voice. "I remember our wife saying something about what she wanted for her wedding night."

Ivy gave a shudder and smiled. "Yes," she whispered.

"And we can add ourselves to the Mile High Club as well," laughed Bodhi. "I wonder how many people can claim that." He produced a brand new, large bottle of lube from the bedside table. "I planned ahead," he said with a wink, "and made sure this would be here for us."

Pulling the covers down, they crawled onto the bed. In their eagerness for each other, they were a twisted mass of caressing limbs and busy mouths. Murmured endearments filled the air as they stroked, licked, and nibbled on any body part that was available. Flesh on heated flesh slid and grasped hungrily. Their ardor reached an enormous peak of want as Bodhi finally popped open the bottle, greased up his erection, and handed the bottle to Cooper to do the same. Bodhi lay back on the bed with his upper body propped by pillows and scooted Ivy toward him, facing Cooper's direction. He stroked her clit and in one swift motion, impaled her pussy with his pulsing erection. He was so eager for this to happen he was nearly hyperventilating. Cooper, now lubed up, leaned in and kissed Bodhi and then Ivy deeply and lovingly.

"Ready?" he asked her.

"More than ready," she breathed on a sigh. "Do it, Cooper. Make love to both of us."

Ever so carefully, Cooper slid a finger inside her pussy alongside Bodhi. Bodhi moaned as Cooper caressed his cock up and down. Pulling out and adding even more lube, Cooper went back in, this time with two fingers. Ivy moaned and trembled in Bodhi's arms as he kissed the side of her face and whispered encouragement into her ear.

"Are you trying to tease us?" asked Ivy in a shaky voice. "I need you now, Cooper. *We* need you. Please!"

"I need to make sure you're relaxed enough so that I don't hurt you, babe. You're going to have a lot of dick inside you." His own was so hard and throbbing, he could barely see straight. It begged to get inside, but still he held back until she relaxed even more.

Finally, Cooper probed her entrance with his massive erection. This was going to be a tight fit, so he fed himself in by small increments. Once the whole head was inside, Ivy's eyes flew open and she cried out, "Oh, yes! There it is. Can you feel him, Bodhi? Come on, Cooper, fuck us!"

Just then the plane gave a massive and unexpected jolt because of air turbulence, and Cooper's attempt at going slowly was shot to hell. He pitched forward and rammed his cock inside her with a huge groan. "Sorry! Oh, sorry, Ivy. Are you okay? Ohmygawd, this feels incredible!" Without even really trying, they were jostled and flung about on the bed, all connected and gasping for breath. The plane hit another massive patch of turbulence and they all cried out as they experienced the weightlessness of a falling-elevator sensation for a few seconds.

After she caught her breath, Ivy began moaning, "Yes, yes, yes!" at the same time Bodhi shouted, "Ahh! Right there! Do it some more!"

After a couple more minutes of being flung about like they were riding a roller coaster, the air turbulence disappeared as quickly as it had arrived. They calmed down into a rhythm of gyrations. Ivy squeezed and released her men in time with Cooper's thrusts, and Bodhi reached around to toy with her clit. "It's just like the book said," he rumbled in amazement. "We're all fucking each other at the same time. Ivy, you feel like a fist that's holding our dicks together, and I can feel every inch of Coop rubbing against me. Wow. I don't know who came up with this, but they're a genius."

Although all of them wanted this magnificent ambrosian delight to last forever, excitement and pleasure took over and carried each of them over the edge. One by one, they cried out in amazed rapture as they trembled and shook in each other's arms.

It was only then that they realized there was a lit sign above the door directing them to return to their seats.

"Oopsie," Ivy giggled. And the light in the sign turned off.

* * *

When they looked back on their honeymoon in the years to come, this was the favorite memory they had. It was just too bad that when people asked about their trip, they had to be polite and actually talk about what they'd seen and done in Australia.

Epilogue

As Jackson had requested, Bodhi went to work managing his investments for him, and when Jackson made his second billion dollars, Bodhi didn't even think about looking for more clients. He became an extremely wealthy man, and a professionally fulfilled one as well. Jackson liked that he could trust Bodhi with his wealth, and Bodhi shined with having that trust. He loved working from home in his plush new office so he could keep an eye on the puppy Ivy and Cooper surprised him with.

It was the golden retriever he'd always wanted. He loved her so much, in fact, they got him another. Since he'd named the first pup Bonnie, it only seemed fair to name the next one Clyde and hope they didn't get into too much trouble together. That was debatable.

Ivy delighted her husbands by producing a gaggle of outspoken, brilliant children. She popped them out every couple of years—boy, girl, boy, girl. Each child had such an independent streak, and so many talents, it was a challenge to keep up with them. One thing they all did, however, was learn to surf with their dads.

Bodhi was thrilled to realize his dream of having a little ballerina and went to every one of Sylvie's dance recitals. He often cried at them, making the whole family snicker. He didn't care. And it turned out, she was a great dancer who bore a striking resemblance to her mother with her dark eyes and hair.

Their other daughter Nell was fascinated by Cooper's law practice and used to make her siblings and friends play 'court-room' with her. She went on to join the family law office and became an outstanding trial lawyer. Ivy laughed all the time about how their fiery redhead daughter had turned her talent for arguing into a marketable skill.

Their younger son Brooks became a professional surfer and made quite a name for himself on the international surf-ing competition circuit. Cooper and Bodhi were beside them-selves about his talent and flew around the world to watch him compete whenever they could. He looked remarkably like Bodhi with his thick mop of blond hair and the signature chin dimple, and he made millions endorsing sports products with that face.

Their eldest child Dash had a heart that was steadfast and pure. He fell in love at the age of four with Rhiannon—Willa, Jackson, and Casey's younger daughter—and never wavered from that affection throughout his entire life. He spent an inordinate amount of time with Jackson as well, pestering him good-naturedly for knowledge about computer science, and ultimately, they designed another mega-hit app together. Cooper gave Dash the heirloom engagement ring that he and Ivy had decided against using when they included Bodhi into their union. Dash and Rhiannon's inevitable marriage bonded the two families even more closely together.

It was never a conventional family, but it worked for them.

The End

If you are interested in more MMF reading, please look for these books:
The Rule of 3
Just Curious
The Golden Rush

Acknowledgments

Some of this book was written during an extra difficult time for us, and I have to pay tribute to the compassionate group of doctors and nurses in the ICU of the local hospital. Our event did not have the happy outcome that happened in this story, but it did give me an experience from which I could draw inspiration. Also, in my own way I have hinted at an individual who was near and dear, by incorporating some personality traits in one of these characters.

On the other hand, I'd like to acknowledge someone else who has always been a truly horrible person. I know this sounds odd, but if you have ever experienced the baffling behavior of a pathological liar, some of Blair's behavior will ring true. Lying for the sake of lying is an incredible thing to me, and lying without care for being found out is stupefying. And yet there are those individuals who simply lie for sport and personal gain. For years I watched this behavior play out, never understanding how the individual could keep it up. So, thanks for the inspiration, you creep.

On to happier topics!

I held a contest via my newsletter, inviting readers to come up with a name for the "female villain" in this book, and Blair Hendrix was born. Many thanks to everyone who submitted names and subsequently voted on the top choice out of my list of favorites. Huge thanks and congratulations to Latifa Morrisette for coming up with Blair's name. Having that great name helped me create Blair's personality. I hope you enjoy your free copy of the book, Latifa!

I also need to thank my wonderful team. Susan is my great friend and beta reader who answers all of my weird questions and isn't afraid to tell me when I've messed up. Amy Maranville is my conscientious editor who is brilliant and makes writing fun. And Mattie Davenport, my terrific proofreader, has yet to acknowledge her true level of coolness. Thank you all.

Thank you, readers, for spending this time inside my head. I hope you continue to enjoy it here. Your support means every-thing to me. Each book that is sold or downloaded via Kindle Unlimited feels like an individual victory. And when a book hits the bestsellers list... indescribable!

And finally, thank you to my family for simply being The Best.

If you'd like to stay in touch, please sign up for my newsletter. https://landing.mailerlite.com/webforms/landing/m6f3i7 I generally mail one out once a month.

Also, I love to hear from readers. info@ariellatalix.com

Books by Ariella Talix

Porter the Importer: Prequel to The Drummonds Series
The story of the Drummond family begins with Molly Drummond and Porter Delaney in this prequel novella. Find out how Porter became the Importer and how Molly started her naughty boutique. Fall in love with Porter and the Drummonds.

Make Believe: The Drummonds- Book One
Lily Drummond's emotional love story with Finn Reilly is romantic suspense with plenty of humor and cute dogs. A page-turner! It's a Canterbury Tales-like saga with a host of interesting characters.

The Artist: The Drummonds- Book Two
This is David Drummond's story with Amelia Hernandez. It takes place mostly in Paris, and it will pull at your heartstrings. Imagination and beauty from page to page. A sizzling, sexy love story and much, much more.

Save Her: Lovers in Louisville- Book One
This series is a spin-off from The Drummonds. Your favorite characters appear again in supporting roles. *Save Her* is full of suspense and a couple you will adore. Åse Halvorsen is a beautiful jewelry designer, and Gunnar Dahl is a famous mystery writer with a secret.

Saving Him: Lovers in Louisville- Book Two

Sibylla Eliana Xenopoulos (Sibley) was Åse's roommate and best friend in college. She returns to Louisville for a great opportunity and finds love with Gunnar's buddy Leo Spanos. Their chemistry is off the charts, but danger lurks in the shadows.

Savor This: Lovers in Louisville- Book Three

In this passionate and unpredictable story, Halden Dahl, Gunnar's younger brother, is a successful glass artist and total ladies' man. Handsome and talented with an ego as big as all outdoors, has he finally met his match?

The Rule of 3

Since no one actually lives in Louisville in this book, it became a standalone spin-off from the popular "Lovers in Louisville" series. Tanner Lassiter, Zoë Deliban, and a new character, Eli Whittaker, all make for a delightful book about ambition, loyalty, and the deepest, most enduring kind of love. It's a second-chance, billionaire, small-town, MMF love story.

Just Curious

This standalone MMF story is about Willa, a gorgeous and highly successful writer who falls for her billionaire neighbor Jackson and his life-long friend Casey. An old acquaintance causes them trouble, and the seriousness of it escalates to a dangerous level. The setting is mostly in southern California, but they do some globe-trotting as well.

Compelling Urges

A loose spin-off from *Just Curious*, this MMF story is also set in San Diego County. Bodhi Monaghan, Cooper Houston, and Ivy Chambers navigate some troubled waters before they can manage their life together as a triad. Doubts and trust issues plague them as well as a strange and interesting character who is bent on claiming or possibly ruining Bodhi.

The Golden Rush: Hearts of Gold- Book One
This is an MMF romance set during the 1849 California Gold Rush. Six men travel across the country, creating an unbreakable bond of friendship, and find themselves in the right place at the right time. Jasper Langley and Royal Dawson eventually meet Adeline Hart, and both fall head over heels for her. It is a moving tale of perseverance, compassion, and sheer grit.

Fiddle and Fire: Hearts of Gold- Book Two
The sequel to *The Golden Rush* will be out in 2022.